EDEN SUMMER

EDEN SUMMER

Liz Flanagan

David Fickling Books

SCHOLASTIC INC. / NEW YORK

First published in the United Kingdom in 2016 by David Fickling Books, 31 Beaumont Street, Oxford OX1 2NP.

www.davidficklingbooks.com

"Wind" and "Six Young Men" from COLLECTED POEMS by Ted Hughes. Copyright © 2003 by The Estate of Ted Hughes. Reprinted by permission of Farrar, Straus and Giroux.

Library of Congress Cataloging-in-Publication Data available

ISBN 978-1-338-12120-9

10 9 8 7 6 5 4 3 2 1   17 18 19 20 21

Printed in the U.S.A. 23

First edition, July 2017

Book design by Mary Claire Cruz

In memory of
Ben Flanagan
&
Yvonne Hook
with love

PROLOGUE

Christmas Day • 11:48 a.m.

The snowfall stole color from the valley, leaving it as black and white as an old photo: dazzling fields, leaden skies, winter trees drawn in charcoal. The chapel sat squat and square on top of the hill, guarded by iron gates.

Late morning, two teenagers came trudging up the lane, their clothes shockingly bright against all that white, voices shattering silence.

The words froze on their lips as they reached the grave-yard gate.

One pulled ahead. She plowed awkwardly, knee-deep through the drifts, to the newest grave, to that headstone at the end, not yet weathered, still gleaming under its little hood of snow. The girl pulled off her hat and gloves and bent over the grave, whispering. Her cheeks were pink with cold and shiny with tears.

"Let's make her a snowman," she said, wiping her face. "She always loved them."

They both started rolling and patting and scraping. They made a little rounded figure the same height as the headstone. They gave it arms of fallen twigs. They made a face with stones and leaves.

When they left, the snowgirl stayed, keeping watch all that short day, till the shadows turned lilac, then blue, ash, then finally black, till the stars came out, clear and hard and pure, glittering over the valley.

PART ONE

CHAPTER ONE

8:00 a.m.

That morning I have no clue what's happened. No inkling. No foreboding. Zilch. I must be the opposite of psychic, 'cause I'm actually almost happy.

Mum's radar picks up on it straight away. "Good to hear you singing again, Jess," she says as we wait for the kettle to whistle.

After breakfast I hug her and tumble out into the blue-and-gold morning. Warm, but with proper cold hiding in the shadows ready to ambush you, warning you that summer's nearly done. I love September, always have. The air is crisp, with that first bittersweet scent of autumn. It smells of hope, new pencils and fresh starts.

I put my earbuds in and start my favorite playlist as I hurry down the hill. Town's all laid out in the sunshine like a tourist website inviting you to visit Yorkshire: the tall skinny houses, rows and rows of terraces, clinging to the crazy gradient.

I make myself late 'cause I keep stopping to take photos on my phone: backlit leaves, tangled weeds all dried and seedy, reflections in the canal. Art is the only class I really care about and I'm looking for something to spark the next project.

I have to run for the bus, but I still get a window seat on the top deck, cocooned in warmth. I lean my head on the glass and half close my eyes. The music is a ladder and my mind climbs it slowly, enjoying the view from up there. I barely see what's actually through the window—the familiar hills, flung wide like a dancer's skirts; the farms dotted high along spreading contours; the wooded ravines; and the houses tucked into the valley bottom or ribboning along this road, this crazy over-crowded road that we're all addicted to, 'cause it's the quickest way out of this place.

In the next village, I get off the bus at the stop nearest school, and that's when it happens: The morning's golden bubble shatters like glass.

I see my best friend's mum. Eden's mum, Claire. Her car is pulling out of the side road, barely three feet away. Her face is gray, and her ponytail is coming loose. I've never seen her without makeup before.

Claire should not be driving 'cause she can hardly see: Her face is crumpled, dripping with tears as she grips the wheel. I've seen Claire cry before, but this shocks me to a standstill.

Someone bumps into my back and barges around me. I clutch at the brick wall to my left for balance because the world is tipping sideways.

Before I can dart into the road and knock on the car window, she's moved out into the main road and driven off.

What's happening? What is Claire doing here, looking like that?

My heart clenches coldly.

Pain starts building in my temples. It's been a migraine-free week till now. First in ages. I yank out my earbuds and stab at my phone to silence the music.

One missed call. From Eden's landline. No message. How did I miss it? Must've been boarding the bus.

I call her mobile, breathless. It goes straight to voice mail. "E, it's Jess. What's up? I saw your mum just now, at school. Did she drop you off? Did you two have a fight? Tell me where you are: I'll come find you."

I hurry up the side road toward school, joining the flow of kids all heading that way. As we get near the sprawling brick-and-glass buildings, I realize something's most definitely up. Everyone's staring. Whispering behind hands. Even the lads. Even the oldest ones.

I'm not being paranoid, for once. I glare back, hating them all, hating that it takes me straight back to the worst months of my life. The rest of the school talking *about* me, not *to* me. Eyes shifting sideways before they meet mine, like disaster might be contagious.

I even flick my eyes down just to check I haven't tucked my skirt into my underwear or something. Nope, all present and correct: paint-spattered boots loosely tied with red laces, only slightly torn leggings, black hoodie with sleeves pulled down over my tattoos, skirt twisted sideways, and the crappy green school shirt that makes everyone—'cept Eden—look sick as a dog. I shake my hair forward, over my face. These days I'm rocking Poppy Red again, though I was stuck on Sky Blue for a bit last year and when it faded, there was a weird washed-out stage when I looked like I'd gone prematurely gray. Today I look OK, or as near to that as I'm ever going to get. So what's happening here?

Head down, I hurry toward the left of the buildings. I need somewhere to think, before I can face this. I need to escape all these people staring at me.

I hear snippets of speculation that no one is even trying to keep quiet.

"*She must know!*"

"*Do you think the police will want to talk to her?*"

"*Jess Mayfield and Liam Caffrey. Definitely.*"

Liam is Eden's boyfriend. Hearing our names linked like that is not good. I feel my cheeks burning. On autopilot, I navigate the main driveway, ducking to miss a football. I'm heading for the back route, around the portable classroom extensions so I can slink into the side yard and hide till Eden rings me back.

I take the corner too fast and slam straight into Josh Clarkson, Eden's ex-boyfriend from last year. Josh's arrogance reaches you two feet before he does, just like his aftershave. I never got what Eden saw in him, except they matched in a tall, golden, pretty kind of way. Till he opened his mouth.

"Look, lads. If it in't Mayfield the gloomy goth girl." Josh flicks his cigarette away. "Miserable mosher. No wonder she looks so beat-up."

He tosses the long hair out of his eyes and sneers at me. "You're some shit magnet, you know that?" He takes a step closer. "You're a freak, your mum's a lezzer, and now your best mate's missing."

They surround me, Josh and the three mates he keeps to make him look good. They've all bought into the same weird posture and overstyled hair, like they're expecting to be kidnapped into some low-rent boy band any day now.

Maybe it was a mistake coming this way. There's no one to see what happens. To my right, the wall of the extension. To my left, an overgrown hedge and the fence behind. It's like a corridor—with escape up ahead too far away.

They start crowding me. The pain in my head ratchets up. I use deep, slow breathing to keep control. I concentrate on the feel of a small stone on the tarmac pressing into the base of my boot.

"Lost your better half? Eden Holby's not so perfect now, is she?"

Tick, tick, tick . . .

Precious seconds slip by. Whatever's happened, Eden will need me. I need to find out. I need to move.

"She was asking for it, Eden Holby. On self-destruct." Josh Clarkson smiles, slow and wide, trying to seem wolfish or something. "No way *she's* gay—you won't turn that one. Always liked it dirty, know what I mean?"

The hyena boys start baying. "What do you want, Clarkson?" My voice hardly wobbles at all.

"If Eden's missing, Liam Caffrey did it, no question. Is that what you'll tell the police?"

This is going too fast for me. I can't take it in. What's he going on about Liam for? I can see why Josh hates him, though. Liam's got Eden now. Plus, he's everything Josh will never be.

"Get lost." I screw my eyes closed and hold my breath and march forward. Maybe I look weird enough to win some space, 'cause when I open them again, the side gate is closer, and my way is clear.

"Ask Caffrey where he hid the body!" Clarkson bawls after me, so loud the whole school can hear him. "Go on, ask him, why don't you?"

Liam would never hurt Eden. The idea is so ridiculous I could laugh.

As I scuttle toward the safety of school, I can't help noticing stupid details all around me: an empty chips packet blowing past; the smell of the freshly mown grass; the way the sky is reflected in the school windows, a lovely deep blue with fluffy clouds.

And then it hits me: Liam could hurt Eden. Liam *has* hurt Eden. And I'm the only one who knows.

CHAPTER TWO

8:35 a.m.

"E, it's me again! Please . . . Listen, I don't care where you are. I'll come find you. Just call me back, OK?"

Eden Holby. Eden Holby. Everyone's saying her name. I hear it on repeat, like emergency news headlines on the TV screen, cutting across everything else.

Somehow I make it into registration, but our homeroom teacher, Mr. Barwell, isn't there. There's some nervy stand-in who can't keep control. This makes it worse. The chaos in our homeroom mirrors the panic rising inside me.

I gulp down headache pills, hoping I'm in time to stop it turning blinding. Today is too important to be eaten up by a migraine. I need to stay alert.

I know everyone's still talking and staring as we take our seats, but it reaches me distantly.

"Where's Eden Holby?"

"Hey, goth girl, where's yer mate?"

I feel like I'm underwater. Everything's muffled. I think a few of them—Ebonie, Sam, Amir—try to be kind. I watch their mouths moving, but I can't work out what they expect me to say.

I sit stiffly, clutching my bag and my phone, ready to bolt. The seconds slouch by. My eyes flick from the clock on the wall to the display on my phone, and the substitute teacher doesn't dare tell me off for using it in class.

"Sir, excuse me, sir? Jess Mayfield has to go to Trent's, I mean, Mrs. Trent's office, sir." The little Year Seven kid disappears almost before he's finished the message, and I'm out of there without waiting for the nod.

I throw myself down the empty corridor. Out into light. Speed across the yard. Concrete stairs. Two at a time. Back inside. Main doors. I'm there.

In the corridor outside Trent's office, I find Imogen and Charlotte heading the same way. Eden's other friends. The ones from the top academic track. The ones who match her in swagger and style.

Imo has black hair extensions down her back, huge eyes, and perfect dark brown skin. Charlotte has a glossy little bob, and while she's usually as pale white as me, this summer's fake tan is fading out: I see the tide marks around her hairline. Her eyebrows are plucked so high that she always looks vaguely surprised, but I think she actually means it right now.

They don't often speak to me. We're different planets, orbiting Eden. But today we're spinning off course and it makes us collide.

"Hey, Jess," Imo says. "Isn't it awful? I couldn't believe it when Eden's mum called me before school." She manages to make this all about her, as usual, letting us know that she was the one Claire turned to first. "Do you think Eden's OK?"

"I mean, we knew she was drinking too much . . . ," Charlotte chips in, watching to see how I react. "We were just talking about that."

"Do you think she had a problem with it?" Imo takes a quick furtive look around us. "I mean, it's understandable and everything, but was it out of control?" She whispers it confidentially, as if she's giving me something precious, and I resist the urge to slap her.

The school trip—five days in July—surfaces in my mind, and I squash it down again. They were there, Imogen and Charlotte, but they didn't have a clue. Anyway, Eden didn't have a problem. Except the obvious. She was drunk and sad, that was all.

"No," I say firmly. But another memory rises up, evidence for the prosecution, and this one takes more effort to push away.

CHAPTER THREE

8:45 a.m.

I appear to have killed their attempt at conversation, distracted by bad memories. The three of us stand in silence, facing Trent's door. To try to get a grip, I use an old trick of Mum's. She says, *However bad things are, make a list of three things you can do about it. Doesn't matter how small.*

Right now it's:

1. *Get in there*
2. *Find out the facts*
3. *Ring Eden again, soon as*

I focus on the door: smooth, dull gray, with a neat little printed sign, PRINCIPAL, MRS. C. TRENT, and a panel of fireproof glass. Right now it's holding back something terrible and I don't want to open it.

I imagine the bad news trapped inside, like a fire. I picture myself opening the door. . . .

Whoomph! The air is devoured. The smoke pours out, hot and choking. Flames erupt, faster than thought, tearing up the walls.

I blink.

I reach out to knock.

Before I can make contact, the door opens from the inside and I stumble forward. My hands land on Liam Caffrey's chest. Warm cotton. I swear I can feel his heart.

I pull back as if I'm scalded.

It's the first time I've seen him close up all week. I think he's been avoiding me. My body reacts, even now, betraying me. My legs turn unsteady. My palms are sweating and my heart goes mad.

He doesn't look like Liam. Nothing gorgeous about him now. Hulking in that doorway, he seems to fill more space than usual. His short fair hair is tufted up, like horns. His face is scrunched up so tightly I can hardly see his eyes. His eyebrows are knotted tight, telling me to back off. I can feel the anger coming off him in hot waves, and I flatten myself against the wall instinctively. For a split second, I am afraid of him.

Then the questions crowd in, and I choose the two at the front. "Liam, what's going on? What did she say?"

But Liam stalks past us in silence. He grabs the outer door handle and wrenches it open so hard it bites into the wall, sending little white crumbs of plaster flying.

I've never seen him so angry. What has she said to him?

"Jess? Is that Jess Mayfield?" Trent appears, and I can see she's rattled. She tugs at her navy suit jacket, pats her cropped gray hair, then fumbles for the glasses resting on her formidable chest. She puts the glasses on and peers at a sheaf of papers in her hand.

It shocks me to notice the whole lot is trembling.

"Jess? Come in. Charlotte, Imogen, wait there. I won't be long, girls."

I don't move. I can feel the other two staring at me.

"Jess? I *said*, come on in. It's all right, Jess, it's only me and Mr. Barwell." Trent beckons me forward.

I peer inside.

Barwell's OK. In the past, he's proved he's human and I can trust him.

"Morning, Jess." He sighs his words out and nods, beckoning me in. He looks terrible.

I go in. It's warm, too warm, with sunlight pouring through the glass walls of the room. It feels like a goldfish bowl. Don't goldfish die if they get too hot? This feels suffocating.

I flop onto one of the empty chairs on this side of the desk—I can feel the coarse padded weave of it through my leggings. I know this place well. I've been here a lot this past year.

Trent shuts the door and takes her seat.

Barwell clears his throat and says the words that change everything. "Jess, I'm really sorry to have to tell you this, but Eden didn't come home last night."

CHAPTER FOUR

9:00 a.m.

"No!" I shake my head. Even after seeing Claire this morning, I don't want to believe it. I see it in the teachers' faces too: the unbelievable cruelty of it. If this was a TV soap, they'd've laughed it off for being too grim—*No, not the same family. No one will believe that. It's too much.*

And it is too much for me. In the heat and light of Trent's office, everything shimmers. I wonder if I'm going to pass out.

Barwell asks me gently, "Jess, do you understand?"

Trent takes over, living up to her nickname: the Tank. Barging in, crushing any last shreds of hope. "Mr. and Mrs. Holby have reported Eden missing. It seems she didn't come home last night. The police have launched an investigation."

I stare at her, trying to read the truth here. Trent is sitting as straight as the blue ring binders in a stiff row edging her desk. She's as composed as her neat pile of papers. Do they have training in this? How to keep control of yourself and everyone else when one of your students is bloody missing? I imagine grabbing her by her suit jacket shoulders and shaking her till that tortoisey neck wobbles.

"But I saw her. I left her at the bus stop. Last night, same as always." I remember Eden's plans. "Ask Liam! Didn't he tell you? She was out with him last night—he'll put you right." This is stupid. They must have made a mistake. We can sort this out if we all just talk to each other.

"She didn't come home last night, although Mrs. Holby did receive a text message this morning," Barwell says, earning a glare from Mrs. Trent as if he wasn't supposed to tell me that.

"So she's not missing?" I blurt. "If she texted, she's not missing. What's everyone panicking for?"

Why didn't she text me? A squirm of guilt spirals through my guts.

"I don't get it." I shake my head. "What does that even mean? She didn't come home? So she might've stayed out. That's not a crime, is it?"

Eden's next to me, laughing at the misunderstanding, tilting her head sideways and rolling her eyes. She flicks her hair back and extends one hand to me.

I blink. Eden vanishes.

I look sideways at Barwell. He's edgy, can't sit still. He ruffles his short dark hair with one hand and I see the silver in it gleaming like wire. His concern tells me this is real. It's right to be scared.

"Jess, I know this is awful. It's a complete nightmare, for the Holbys, for you, for the school, for us." Barwell speaks with a southern accent, Essex or somewhere. He's one of the rare ones—tough but funny, and you can tell that he cares, deep down. "But we're here for you. The school wants to offer you support."

"Oh my God." I put my hands to my forehead, where the pain is tightening like a snare, trapping me.

"We're all desperately worried about Eden," Trent butts in over us both, sounding not very worried at all, just a bit pissed off at the inconvenience, actually. "But there are systems in place here. We need to stay calm."

So much for offering me support. Her eyes move to my left wrist, where the fabric has risen, showing the newest tattoo. I bring my hands down again, tugging my sleeve low, twisting it in my palm as I squirm on the seat.

"The police investigation has already begun. As you can imagine, it's top priority, after all the Holbys have endured. . . ." Trent coughs. "The thing is, Jess, they will need to speak to you."

I grip the chair so hard that one fingernail snaps.

"I've just spoken to your mother. She's expecting you. You need to go home and wait for the officers to come round. They'll do the interview there and your mother will be with you."

"Now?" I whisper.

Barwell nods.

"It won't take long," Trent tells me briskly. "You can slot back into lessons when you're done."

A faint whine starts up in my ears, like my own personal mosquito. My vision changes: The contrast goes crazy, so

Trent's suit is saturated, dark as an ink spill. The windows are a dazzling blur.

"You can help." Barwell's voice reaches me as though he's shouting across a river, through the rushing in my head. "What you tell the police—that's going to help them find Eden as quickly as possible. OK?"

No. Not OK. Not OK at all.

"Listen, Jess, you're in a special position. More than anyone here, you know Eden. You know how she was. This summer. This week. The last time you saw her."

CHAPTER FIVE

"The *last* time . . . ?" It sounds too final.

I think about the last time I saw Eden, praying with everything I've got that it's not the actual *last* time. It was far too ordinary for that. Ordinary, but not normal. And certainly not happy.

Last night after school, we waited by the overcrowded bus stop—the sheep pens, we call them—trying to ignore the racket of the younger kids. It was always easier, being there with Eden. She's got this thing, like a force field but good, so that when you're with her, you're inside a golden circle and you're safe.

We filed onto the bus, choosing the usual seats halfway down on the left of the top deck. We live in the next town, two miles down the valley, so the bus journey was only ten minutes, if that.

Mostly I like living there, in our little town, the one they call quirky, the one everyone's heard of, with the artists and the lesbians and the eco-mums and the art festival. The one where the last mills standing became little boutique shops the tourists adore, or cafés or galleries—so at least there is somewhere to work. That isn't why I like it, though. I like the hills. The moor. The rivers. How you can be up on the tops in fifteen minutes and see only two other people during the whole run.

Last night I got the window seat and I couldn't stop myself squinting out against the sunshine, searching the faces as the bus pulled away. Then I turned to Eden.

"So, Thursday night . . . ," I said, watching her face carefully. "Got anything lined up?"

We sat there, limp in the heat, drenched in sunlight through the bus window.

Eden shrugged. "Dunno. Usual. Home first. And Liam texted: He wants to meet up. The delights of town await," she ended sarcastically. She tossed her long blond hair over one shoulder, somehow managing to keep it smooth, shiny, and apple-scented, while mine frizzed in red clumps.

I hid my expression by raising my hands, lifting my hair off my hot, damp neck. "Wait, you don't mean hanging in the skate park? And then the club? How can you bear the excitement? Not a real game of pool?"

Our town has just the one club. It isn't bad. Liam's sister Nicci works there, serving us drinks discreetly, and we sit in the bar, playing cliché bingo: one point each for a crossbreed dog, a white man with dreadlocks, and a woman in tie-dye on the dance floor. It has some good nights each month, with bands or DJs, but Thursday night wasn't one of them.

"If Nicci's working, you'll get drinks too. How cou. one resist?" I played along, ignoring the flutter of somethin. my chest, using a silly voice to match her dryness.

"You?" She did that head tilt, looking at me sideways.

"Usual . . . my running night, remember?" I murmured back, closing my eyes against the light so she couldn't see what I was trying to hide.

When had this happened, batting each other away with cover stories? This wasn't a conversation, it was a game of alibis.

"Yep, Thursday equals self-inflicted pain as I try to keep up with the good ones," I mumbled now. I felt too hot. My skirt was sticking damply to my legs. I blew my bangs upward. "Probably do a route up the moor."

"And who says we don't know how to live? You'll be getting hot and sweaty with a dozen lads." She wrinkled her nose. "I wouldn't go for those ones, though—they're like greyhounds, no meat on 'em. . . ."

"I don't go for the lads. I go for the running. It's a hill-running club, Eden." I spelled it out for her, but it came out more harshly than I meant.

She looked at me in surprise, perfect eyebrows arched.

"Look, we're here," I said abruptly, eager to change the subject. The bus was slowing and I rose and grabbed the handrail, so she had to get up.

This was where we usually went our separate ways, at the park gates. I just had to walk through the park and up the steps to our corner of town, where the houses were tightly packed together: town houses, duplexes, the old public housing flats.

On our street, you knew your neighbors' names and what they yelled when they had fights. I liked it: It made me feel safe, hearing doors slam, the faint meow of next door's baby through the wall, kids kicking a ball outside the garages.

Eden had to wait for one of the little minibuses that went up the steeper hills. She lived in a massive stone farmhouse up on the tops.

"Farm, my arse," she said when they first moved there. "No chance of us getting a cat, never mind any proper farm animals. They like the idea of a farm. They want to buy designer Wellingtons and a four-wheel drive. Then they'll pay someone else to do the yard."

We leaned on the wall next to the bus shelter. The stone was warm through my shirt. We got black looks from two old dears with shopping bags who glared at Eden's minuscule skirt and sandals, my makeup and hair, as if it offended them just to see us.

"I can wait with you," I said after a moment, feeling like I'd snubbed her. I was supposed to be looking out for her, not getting snappy. I was Eden's best friend and she'd had the year from hell. Eden and me both. It's like we were on a seesaw, up or down, never even but somehow balanced. Right now she was farther down, while I was on the up. So it was my turn to be there for her, and that meant taking any kind of crap.

"You don't have to," she said.

I rolled my eyes.

"I mean, thanks." Eden stabbed at her phone. "But Liam should be meeting me soon."

"I'll take off, then, leave you to it." I peeled myself off the warm stone and hoisted my bag onto my shoulder.

"What's going on with you two?" she asked sharply.

"Nothing's going on." I kept my voice as level as I could, praying the flare of heat in my cheeks didn't show.

She glanced at me sideways. "Just seems like you've been avoiding him." Her voice was deceptively light. I knew her too well to fall for it.

I shrugged. "Why would I do that?" I faced her, searching her expression for clues. "It's just harder for us all to hang out, now summer's done. School gets in the way."

"Yeah, but why . . . ?" she began, when something pinged into her inbox. Something more important than me. Saved by the bell. Eden grinned widely, happy as a cat in sunshine, staring at her phone as if it was made of rubies.

I didn't ask. In my head I was busy burying something, piling soil, filling a hole, packing it down. It was hard work, but soon I'd be done.

Around us, people stirred into life, picking up bags, moving toward the curb. Sure enough, the little bus was trundling down the main street. It stopped with a wheeze of warm air, and people started climbing aboard.

"Have fun later." I forced a smile back at her, even though my face felt stiff with deceit. "See you." I did a funny wave to show everything was OK between us. A wave that lied. A wave that wished it was true.

Eden laughed and got on the bus, all shining blond hair and long tanned legs. The double doors closed, swallowing her up.

CHAPTER SIX

9:35 a.m.

Trent stands up, signaling she's finished with me. "Off you go, Jess. Don't worry. I fully expect Eden to be home soon."

Her tone doesn't fill me with hope.

"She's had a hard time, that's all. Since June. *Since Iona . . .*" She leaves it hanging and her hard face melts a little, into the "sympathy" pose.

I've noticed how hard it is for people to say words like: *Death. Died. Killed. Dead.* I've stood next to Eden and listened to people pussyfooting around it with *passed away.* Or *your loss.* Or *about your sister.* Or *since Iona.*

If she's got to live with it, surely the least they can do is face the truth of it. It's like they are dirty words.

"Yes, it *has* been hard for Eden since her sister *died.*" Understatement of the year. I sound out each word so clearly it comes out a bit unhinged, but I'm sick of it. They know exactly what happened.

28

"You say that," I snap, impatient with Trent's fake sympathy, "but what have you done to help? I mean, really?"

Trent bristles.

I plow on, using my anger. "You're no good in a crisis." I glare at Trent, then shoot Mr. Barwell a tight smile so he knows it's not directed at him. "I don't mean you, sir." I sigh and turn back to her. "You're so busy worrying how the school appears, what the parents think, what the exam results say. A really good school should care when things go wrong. Not make you feel like a problem. To be fixed."

I didn't mean to say that, but it feels better now that it's out.

Barwell is the one who replies, though. Of course. "This isn't about Eden now, is it? Jess, I'm sorry if you feel that the school has let you down."

It is about Eden. Today is all about Eden. But now I've started . . . "You know what, while we're all being so honest? Yeah, I did feel let down back then. But it's not about me. It's about anyone who's a bit different, or having a tough time. You let them all down, and you need to sort it out—"

"I don't think—" Mrs. Trent tries to interrupt, staring down at me.

"Why didn't you say?" Barwell silences her with a gesture, half rising from his chair, then sitting down again and leaning toward me. "Jess, you could have told me."

"Why didn't you see? Why do you think I skipped school?" I think I'm about to burst into tears, and I can't do that, not here, not now. I avoid his eyes and stare down at my knees.

I curl my hands into fists so the broken nail digs into my palms, and it helps. "I wasn't in a fit state to *articulate my needs.*" I say the last bit in a tight voice, channeling Mum. "Don't you see: It's when things are tough that it's hardest to tell someone. It was for me, anyway, and it must be true for Eden or else we'd've seen this coming." I sway in my seat, dizzy with the unfamiliar thrill of telling teachers the truth. "You need to think about what it's like, coming back to school after something bad. You'd better get it right for Eden next week."

Trent sits back down, opening and closing her mouth, more like a tortoise chewing lettuce now.

I've had enough of them both. There isn't time for this stuff now. The heat in the room is suffocating and I can't stand it a second longer.

"I need to go. It's too hot." I stand up in a rush, pushing the chair so hard it tumbles backward. I yank the door open and run through it, past Imogen's and Charlotte's question-mark faces.

Trent starts shouting after me. "Jessica Mayfield, don't you—"

"No, it's all right, Celia. I'm Jess's homeroom teacher. Let me see her out."

Barwell catches up to me by the outside door and puts his weight against it, holding it closed. "Jess, wait. Are you OK?"

Stupid question. I try to settle my breathing and think around my fear. Because it's him, I stop and I wait and I speak patiently. "I'll be all right in a minute," I manage to gasp.

"Don't worry, Jess. The police will find her. Listen, when Eden's back and it's all calmed down, we're going to talk about what you just said. And the school will help, I give you my word. You *and* Eden. OK?"

I nod, to make him feel better. I can't think about that now.

"Good luck with the police." Barwell reaches out as if he plans to squeeze my shoulder, and maybe that would be OK with someone else, but not me. Never me. He remembers, pulls back, and opens the door for me with a sigh. "It shouldn't take too long. I'll see you at registration this afternoon? Come to the teachers' lounge if you need me before then. I mean it."

"OK. Thanks, sir." I stumble outside, blinking fast, straight into the chaos of break time. I feel the weight of Barwell's gaze on my back, like an itch I can't scratch. I check my phone. Its blankness makes me want to scream and hurl it across the yard.

Eden, where are you? Eden, what did you do?

I need to understand how it happened. How we got to today. How the cracks appeared. Then I can use it to work out where Eden is. I should've known, so I have to fix it. I think back to the first time she told me something wasn't right. It was back in April. Back when her sister was still alive.

* * *

I planned my first tattoo for weeks. All through the Easter holidays, I doodled variations before settling on the perfect one. I still wasn't drawing, not properly, but somehow this was OK: small and technical enough to fly under the radar, which told me my inner artist was still broken. I redid the artwork twenty times to get it right. Me and Mum had the fight again one last time the night before.

"What about hepatitis?"

"I told you. That's old news. Get with the twenty-first century, Mum. They use gloves and a new needle each time. Sterile, vacuum-sealed, look!" I spun the laptop round so she could read the FAQs that filled the screen.

"Are you really sure, Jess? It's such a big step. I know people have removals, but it's basically forever. How do you know how you're going to feel? What if you change your mind when you're twenty, or forty? Or sixty?"

"Mum. I'm sure. That's the point. That it's forever, and that I'm sure. That's why it means something. Why can't you see? And it's my body." I used that line a lot.

"Yes, it's your body. And after everything your poor body's been through, I don't understand why you'd give it more pain." She was shouting now, her eyes shining.

"But that's my choice to make. It's *mine!*" I yelled back. "It's the opposite of what they did to me. That's exactly why I'm doing it, honest. I promise you, it's important to me. It's not some whim." I was speaking more earnestly now. I didn't want to upset her. I just needed her to see. "It's going to help me—more than all those counseling sessions put together. You have to believe me." Sometimes I didn't even know I believed something till I found myself arguing it through with Mum. "This is not another problem. This is me getting better."

"How do you know?" she snapped.

I stared her down.

She sighed. "I'm sorry, sweetheart." She gave a little sob and grabbed my hand. "OK! OK! You win. If you really want it, you do it. I don't even know why I'm fighting it. I'm so glad to have you here in one piece, I shouldn't mind if you tattoo every inch of your precious skin. Come here, love."

After our hug she pulled back and looked at me. "But if it's really you getting better, no more skipping school. Deal?"

I recognized that jut of her chin. Yep, she cared, but nope, she'd never be a pushover.

I told Eden all of this as she walked with me down to the tattoo studio, down the quiet end of the longest street in town, next to the yoga place and the garages.

"So she gave you the full Sarah Mayfield?" Eden teased lightly. She knew all about my mum.

"Yep, the full treatment. Talked her into it, but she bargains hard. Perfect attendance from now on."

Eden gave me one of her sideways glances, checking that I was OK. "Sounds like a fair deal."

"Oi." I elbowed her gently. "Whose side are you on?"

"Yours! Always. Thing is, I like it when you're there, at school. I've missed you." And she smiled to soften her words. "Here it is."

My legs unhelpfully turned to cheese strings as we arrived at the door. The studio was on the first floor, signposted by a massive hanging board covered in Celtic designs. I stopped, staring up at it.

"Ready?" Eden asked. "We can still walk away, anytime you like, you know."

"I'm not changing my mind." I glared at her.

"Knew you'd say that. Just checking."

I shook my head, pushed the door open, and started climbing the wooden stairs. Inside it smelled strange: like ink and something strong and chemical.

We reached a light, airy space at the top of the stairs. Bright sunshine streamed in, so the posters on the walls gleamed and dazzled. The woman leaning on the counter watched us without speaking. She had her hair in one of those old-fashioned rolls at the front, wrapped in a spotted scarf, and her eyes were thickly ringed in liquid eyeliner. I made a mental note of the way she'd done that. She wore a bright-pink floral dress, fifties style, and her arms were covered in old-school tattoo work: large roses and leaves.

A man came out from a back room to join her: slightly taller, bald, with a goatee, and his ears pierced with those round discs that look like rubber coins. His bright blue eyes checked us out.

They waited, not hostile, but not welcoming, either.

I held it together, knowing both of us had passed for eighteen before, even without the borrowed ID I was clutching in my sweaty palm.

"Hi. I made an appointment for twelve thirty. I've brought a picture of what I want." I pulled out the artwork to show them, after I'd flashed the ID. "Can you do this? Down my arm?" I'd worked on it for ages—red poppy heads and falling petals, lush and bright.

"Who did this?" the man asked.

"Me." I stared back.

"It's good."

"Thanks."

"You got any more like this?"

"Yeah, plenty." I felt the atmosphere change. "So can you? I mean, will it work?"

"Yeah, that red, though . . . It'll have to be one I mix myself. Come in; I'll show you what I mean . . ." and he held a curtain aside.

I wobbled through. Eden followed. We were in! My heart was beating so fast I had to concentrate hard to think over it.

"Here's what I mean about the red—this one's closest. Right?"

I nodded, mouth too dry to speak. He was right. I knew he was good. I'd read the reviews.

"You doing art at college, is it?" And with that, it was like a cloud moved from the sun: He didn't exactly smile, but his eyes were warm and they focused on me. "I'm Mo."

"Jess."

"Eden."

We talked a bit and I made up stories about my life, as I wanted it to be three years from now, hoping I wasn't jinxing it with the lies. Eden smiled, listening.

Mo said, "Why don't you come by some time? Bring your portfolio. You could work up some new designs for us."

I looked at him hard to check he wasn't mocking me. I shrugged and nodded, as if that wasn't a big deal.

The back room had a huge window, so the light was good, and that reassured me. Then I saw the chair—a massive black leather job, a bit like the one at the dentist's—and I almost bolted.

I managed to sit down and wriggle my left arm out of my T-shirt, pushing bra and cami straps aside, telling myself the guy saw naked skin every day of his working life. "Here?" I traced the line from my shoulder to my elbow. My skin looked blank and pale as a new sheet of white paper.

"That works," Mo agreed.

I sat tense and upright.

"I usually draw it on first, check we're both happy?" Mo said, holding up a ballpoint pen.

I nodded, bracing for the contact. The pen touched my skin. I felt sick. I breathed in, slow and calm.

Mo felt it. "You OK?"

I nodded, steely. It didn't count. It wasn't touch. It was a pen. I was the paper. I knew all about that. "I'm fine." And somehow I was. I even made him draw it three times, till it was perfect.

Then came the needle.

"Ready?" Mo said.

"Yeah," I told him. Then I gasped.

Without asking, Eden held out her hand for me to grab, and kept talking. "D'ya think it'll get addictive? Y'know, you'll come back each year, till you look like you're dressed with nothing on?"

I gripped her fingers tightly. "Dunno. Start small, I reckon. Now I know how much it hurts . . ." I talked through my teeth, breathing the sting away.

The needle burred away, spattering ink. The pain was hot and small. A five out of ten. I knew what ten felt like, and this was nothing.

"What do you want, J? I can talk, or I can shut up. Your call. I've downloaded all sorts—film, last night's TV. I've got quality gossip, been saving it all week."

My gratitude swelled, almost broke into tears. "Beyond the call of duty, E." She'd been like this all year. Eden gave me what I needed, before I even knew what it was. Brought my schoolwork round every single night, walking that steep mile in all weathers when I was still off.

"Yeah, well. What are friends for?"

I squeezed her hand so hard that her knuckles were bruised by the time we finished.

Afterward we went to the riverside café. It was just about warm enough to sit out. The water rushed past, a comforting background constant, like white noise. I could see ducks paddling across the weir and the metal sculpture on the overgrown island turned silver-gold in the cool spring sunshine.

"Cheers for coming with me," I said to her as we sipped our juices. My whole arm buzzed, hot and tender, but the joy rose up, pure and clear, every time I thought of the half-finished design hidden under the gauze. I was tempted to whip out my ice cubes and press them on my arm. "I did it, E! I finally did it."

"Yeah, you did good," she said. "And he wants you to design for him: nice one!" Then, after a pause, "I'm kinda jealous."

"I knew it, you do want one!" I crowed, though it wouldn't really go with her look. "Hey, I could draw something, just for you. . . ."

"Not that." She was serious now, looking down her straw and playing with her drink.

"Eden, what?" I looked over at her, feeling my smile slipping away.

My best friend, the one who had it all: looks, brains, and confidence. We didn't match, me and Eden. We started the same and grew up different. Eden was tall and blond and model-perfect. I was short and skinny and pale, with added color and piercing. My mum thought I was a goth. I'd been called worse.

It didn't matter that Eden and I were mismatched: We just got each other. We knew each other so well: the big stuff and the small. I knew her favorite food (sticky toffee pudding, but always with ice cream, never custard) and why she didn't like spiders (haunted by an incident at Charlotte's party when we were ten) and what she'd choose from the sale rack (anything blue, to match her eyes). We understood each other; we made each other laugh. That was all. That was everything.

Till now.

Now I had no idea what she meant. "*You?* Jealous?"

"Yeah, of you. Marching in there with a picture you drew, knowing you'll never regret it." She still didn't meet my eye. "You're so brave. And strong. Even after what happened. Especially then. Knowing what you want and who you are."

I stared at her, astonished. "So do you!"

"No. That's where you're wrong. I only have negatives. Minus wishes."

"E, what are you going on about?" I asked gently, leaning in and wincing as my shirt caught on the dressing.

"I only know what I *don't* want. I want Iona to get off my case and stop being a bitch. I don't want to mess up the exams. I don't want to disappoint Mum and Dad anymore. I want them to stop looking at me like I'm a freak who ate their perfect little girl. . . . But if you ask me what I actually want, I haven't got a clue."

"That's not true—" I started, but she hadn't finished.

"You've got your mum who loves you: *a lot*. Your running that you love: *a lot*. You want to go to art school: *a lot*. You will, because you're talented: *a lot*. You worked at getting better: *a lot*. You wanted this tattoo: *a lot*. I bet you know exactly what your next hair color will be too, because you've thought about it: *a lot*."

I sat back, feeling picked on, smoothing away a tendril of dyed red hair. "So what are you saying, E? Is my hair color a big deal now?"

"Not just that, no. But if you add it all up, it's a life. I'm drifting along, trying to please people, but it's like I'm a shadow, Jess. You're a real person, and I'm just . . . nothing."

I stared at her, shocked. Then I got up and went around the table and pulled her up, made her stand. I grabbed her and hugged her hard. "Don't you say that, Eden Holby. You're not *nothing*. No one thinks that and you shouldn't neither. You're my best friend and you seem pretty proper to me, all right? Ouch!"

She was hugging me back and it banged my tattoo, and then we were both laughing, even though I could see her eyes shining.

CHAPTER
SEVEN

10:10 a.m.

I leave school in a daze and go home with the memories swimming through my mind. I find the next three steps along the way:

1. *Talk to Mum*
2. *Talk to the police*
3. *Talk to Eden's folks*

This keeps me together till my key's in the door. Then here, in my hallway, I feel safe. Everything looks as it should: worn wooden floor, yellow walls, my running coat hanging limply on the hooks next to Mum's smart jacket. I peek into the kitchen and through to the living room. It's calm and tidy. I hear the kitchen clock ticking and notice a curl of steam above the kettle. Fluff is dozing in a patch of sunshine, and only one ear twitches when I shout, "Hello? Mum?" I hate to admit it, but my cat is getting old: twelve years since I chose that stupid name for him.

"Mum?"

I can hear the burble of Mum's voice in her office above me. Either she's got a client in there or she's on the phone.

She's a *coach, not a therapist* she always says, even though no one else knows the difference. She used to cut hair and listen. Then she retrained, and now the listening pays better, I think. People pay to talk to her. It must help, 'cause they usually come back. Half her work is corporate, coaching business types to greater success, or maybe just helping them accept there's no escape from their boring dead-end jobs. The other half is for charities, like down at the women's shelter. I can tell which kind of day it is by what she's wearing: lipstick and a dark suit, power jewelry; or faded jeans, no makeup, and an unthreatening cardigan.

I don't mind: It seems like an OK job to do. It pays the bills, helped by what Dad sends. I just hate it when we're talking and she forgets I'm her daughter, not a client, keeps asking those positive questions—"How do you want it to be? What do you want to achieve?"—as if everything can be solved through wishful bloody thinking.

She and I both know that's not always true.

On the plus side, she listens well. It's what she's trained to do. Also, she's never minded about the ever-changing hair color. She made me explain myself, and then told me which hair dye would hold best.

And maybe it's easier, just me and her. She split up from Dad when I was three, came out as a lesbian not long after.

That's so not a big deal in our town. Anyway, I don't remember anything different.

I go see Dad most half-terms and two weeks each summer. He married Rachel ages ago and they've got the twins. Hope and Esther are five years old and never stop talking or moving unless they're actually asleep. I love them. I love being a big sister, even though I suspect they see me more like a cousin. Remembering Eden and Iona's fights, maybe that's not such a bad thing.

I love Dad and Rachel's cramped London flat too—in a dark redbrick building with white plasterwork like icing around the door and windows—full of life and color and mess and noise. I love the streets near their house, full of people no matter what time of day it is. I love that you could do almost anything and no one would bat an eyelid. If I ran naked down a street in London, it'd be like chucking a pebble into the Thames: gone in a second. If I did that here, it would be around school in five minutes and the rumors would stick till the day I died.

But I also love leaving London. Coming home. Here, to my house, to my room, where everything stays where I leave it. To Mum. To Fluff. To my art. To the running club. To Eden.

I go upstairs. I can hear Mum's voice speaking softly now, so I can't make out the words. I tiptoe closer to her door. Her voice gets clearer. It's not a work call. She's talking about Eden.

". . . Yes, since last night. The police are on their way here right now. We're next on the list. Yes . . . Claire rang here just after Jess left. God knows what she's thinking. Going through hell again: the police, the waiting. That poor woman. It defies belief. Why do these things happen . . . ?"

There's a pause. Who's at the other end? Must be Steph, her girlfriend.

"I know, I know. You're right . . . Yes, please. I'm going to need the company. Just let me check with Jess first."

I hear the warmth in her voice. I know I'm the reason Steph hasn't moved in yet, when they've been together four years. So far, I've not done anything about it. One day soon I will. I like Steph: It's not that. I didn't want to give up me and Mum, just us, together. Not this year.

"No, you're right. Thanks. Poor Jess. It brings it all back. . . . *Jess*."

I freeze. I shouldn't be listening, but I can't seem to move.

". . . Still feel so bad. It's just . . ." Her voice is thick with held-back tears. It moves to a higher pitch. "I know I couldn't have stopped it. That it's not my fault. Everyone tells me that. But I'm her mum. She's still only sixteen: I should be able to keep her safe."

I can't bear to hear this. I creep back to my room and yell, "Mum!" even louder before slamming my bedroom door really hard.

She comes out and I meet her at the top of the stairs. It's a cardigan-and-jeans day, and her hair's in a loose knot with a pencil stuck through it, streaked blondish strands around her face. She looks tired and her eyes are watery. She opens her arms to me and I throw myself into them. She's my mum, the safe place, the contact I can handle.

"Oh, Jess." She strokes my hair. "Was it awful?"

I nod into the softness of her gray cardigan, breathing in the comfort of her.

"I'm so sorry, sweetheart. I can't believe it either. And you saw her just last night, right? You know the police need to talk to you? They're on their way here right now."

"I know. Oh, Mum."

She pulls back and wipes my cheek with her thumb. "It's going to be OK. You can do this. I'll be here with you the whole time."

I nod.

"What did school say? Let's go down; I'll make us some tea."

"Dunno," I tell her as we go downstairs. "They're being weird about it."

"What do you mean, love?" She presses the button and the kettle starts boiling, steaming away and fidgeting on its base. She lifts down the teapot, takes off its lid.

"Like they know something I don't. There was some text that Eden sent her mum early this morning, and no one will talk about it." I sit down at the kitchen table and put my head in my hands. The pills are working: The headache's faded to a dull throb.

"You've tried ringing her?" She goes to the fridge and gets out a bottle of milk.

"All the time. And texting. I think something's happened."

I look up in time to see Mum tense up. She's reaching the mugs down from the shelf and she pauses halfway. "What about that boy? Has anyone talked to him?" She busies herself with the boxes of tea—about ten different kinds jammed on top of the microwave—and I can see the tension in her jaw, clenching tight when the words are bitten out. "I know something happened last weekend. You weren't yourself, last Sunday, Monday. What happened, Jess? What did he do?"

"*Mum!*" I don't believe it. "*That boy?* You mean Liam? He's my *friend*." That word does nothing to sum up what he is to me, but my anger saves me from the awkwardness. I use it to counterattack. "You *know* Liam. You let him sleep here, under your roof. You weren't jumping to conclusions then!"

Those nights in the summer when Eden didn't want to go home and I knew that, for her sake, Mum would be cool with the three of us all crashed in a big pile of sleeping bags on my bedroom floor.

"Maybe I shouldn't have let him stay. Maybe we don't know enough about him."

"That's bull. You've known Sharon for years. She's like, four streets away." I like Liam's mum. You know where you are with Sharon. You can knock on her door anytime. "What's changed?"

This isn't like Mum, and it starts ice crystals growing inside me. Mum's the kind who bends over backward to believe the best of anyone. "Have you heard something?" Is it the parent grapevine, whispering rumors? "If you have, you'd better tell me!"

She gives up on the tea and turns round. "I'm worried sick, Jess. For Eden and for you. Isn't that enough?"

"Here we go again," I sigh. It took ages for her to get back to normal after the attack last November. She went into mother-wolf mode, über protective. She still didn't like me walking back alone after dark. Running was OK: She let me do that, after the doctor said it was good therapy. Otherwise it was chaperones and taxis all the way, a daily inquisition about where I was going and who I'd be with.

The worst thing is, I know it's not her style. She used to be laid-back, before. I hate that they've done this to her.

The doorbell sounds.

CHAPTER EIGHT

10:35 a.m.

Mum turns, tense and pale. "Be strong. We can do this." She drops a careful kiss on the top of my head and goes to open the door.

I sit there, the blood pounding in my temples. I hear Mum greeting the police, their formal introductions, their steps in our hallway, getting louder.

"Jess? These officers have come to ask you some questions about Eden, OK, love?" Mum's using a bright, fake voice. This brings back bad memories for us both: police in our kitchen.

I'm staring at my white knuckles, but somehow I pull my gaze up and toward them. It's not the same ones as back then.

Two women. One Mum's age, white, with light-brown hair tied back and glasses that make her look like an owl. One younger, Asian, pretty, with a sleek black bob. They're both wearing suits, not uniforms, and I know from TV that it's not a good sign.

The officers flash their IDs and say their names and ranks. Meanwhile, Mum puts a mug of tea in front of each of us on the kitchen table. They pour milk. They don't take sugar.

I need energy right now and stir two sugars in slowly.

They bring out notebooks. They give me smiles that seem carefully calculated to be reassuring. The smiles tell me they're safe. I'm safe. I wonder if the smiles are why they've been chosen for this task.

Mum sits down and the atmosphere changes.

"So, Jess, you know why we're here?" Owl Lady asks.

I can't speak. My throat has closed up.

"Your friend Eden didn't come home last night. We're working very hard to find her as soon as possible. I know you want her home safe, Jess, and so do we. So we'd like to ask you some questions. Your answers could help us find her. Is that all right with you?"

It's a script and she's doing it well. You can tell she's good at her job, but the rehearsed flavor of it spins me out. The clock ticks.

"Jess?" Mum prompts with raised eyebrows.

"Sorry," I manage in a strangled voice. I cough out, "Yeah, but are you sure? Are you sure she's missing? You know she texted her mum? Mr. Barwell said."

The women exchange a quick glance.

"And you? Has Eden been in touch with you?"

"No. Not since yesterday," I say, feeling like a failure of a best friend. "Have you spoken to Liam?" I ask. "He'll tell it straight."

"Liam Caffrey? Eden's boyfriend? We're talking to all of Eden's close friends." Owl Lady is good at deflecting. She's well in control. "Now, Jess," she says firmly, "tell us, please, as much information as you can, even if it seems like a small detail to you. Did anything seem wrong or different with Eden yesterday?"

I shake my head.

"Tell me when you saw Eden last, and how she seemed to you."

I can do that part. I tell them every last detail I can think of.

"And you're sure she was meeting Liam?"

I nod, but then I remember the way she smiled at her phone when it buzzed with something new, and suddenly I'm not so sure. "That's what she said."

"Where would they go?"

"Skate park. Then club. Liam's sister works there. Then he'd walk her home. He did walk her home, right?" I ask.

There's a long beat.

Owl Lady sighs. "OK, Jess, let's get some background. How has Eden seemed lately? Anything unusual in her behavior? Any problems she told you about?"

I stare at them. "You do know her sister just died in June? I'd class that as a problem."

"We know about Iona's death, of course." They nod patiently.

"Has she been finding it harder to cope with that recently?" Sleek Lady takes over, and they alternate smoothly, a slick double act.

"Not really," I say. "I mean, yeah, it's been hard. But

nothing's changed all of a sudden." I'm horrified to find my cheeks getting hotter when I say that.

"Would you say she was depressed?"

"No."

"School? Exams year. Was she feeling the pressure?"

"Nah. She's great with that stuff." Not like me. "She's got an extra subject even."

"Did she talk to you about how she felt?"

"Yes. No. A bit." As I say it, I realize it's been a long time since I knew exactly what was in Eden's head.

They do that glance thing again.

"Eden and Liam—what's that like? How long have they been together?" Owl Lady asks it so lightly and gently that it makes me look at her, surprised.

Why is she suddenly being careful now? It seems like an easy question. Is this one of those questions like on the TV police dramas? Where they know the answer, they're just testing, to see if I can be trusted? Like the first questions on the lie detector tests to establish a base level.

"We've both known Liam for ages, but they met again properly in May." And Eden being Eden, the way they met wasn't something you'd forget in a hurry.

CHAPTER NINE

Shock, horror, it was actually hot on May Day, kicking off the summer in style. I went up to Eden's to hang out. We dragged damp-smelling lounge chairs out of Eden's dad's shed, covered them with beach towels to hide the moldy parts, and made ourselves comfy on the patio in our bikinis. Up there in Eden's garden, you couldn't even see the town tucked away in the valley. It was just us, sheep and lambs baaing madly to each other in the fields, and the whole valley doing its crazy super-green spring thing. I started to feel as if things might be looking up at last.

"SPF fifty for you—catch!" Eden threw a tube of suntan lotion at me.

"All right, all right, so I'm white as a ghost. You don't have to rub it in!"

"Who else is going to do your back, then? *Ta-da!*" She winced at her own crap joke. "'s'all right, you have inner class, you can carry off pale and interesting. Hey, that tattoo is all healed up fine, in't it?"

"Yup. I've already planned the next one too. Been chatting to Mo at the tattoo studio."

"What did he say about your portfolio?"

"Yeah, good. I'm doing a few pages of designs and stuff for them—you know, for people to flick through? They even said they'd pay me if people choose mine." I still found that hard to believe.

She came and sat next to me, and even though it was just Eden, my best friend, I turned to stone.

You can do this, you can do this. . . .

She slopped a cool slick of sunblock onto my shoulder.

I jumped away like it was acid. On my feet, flinching like a kicked mutt.

"Shit, Jess, I forgot." Eden looked horrified.

"It's OK. It's not your fault." I felt stupid. I was sweating and cold at the same time. Mortified. Months now, and I still couldn't cope. I'd hoped it was the end of winter for me on the inside too, but this just showed I was still all frozen up inside.

"Yeah, and it's bloody well not yours, either, and don't you forget it."

"Why don't I do you instead? That should be OK." Somehow it was acceptable to my broken brain for me to touch someone else. I just couldn't handle being touched. Not since . . . Not yet.

"So I did a trial shift at the café yesterday," I said, desperate to change the subject, as she turned her back to me. "Guess who works there."

"No way; I'm not listing our entire school. Just spit it out."

"Liam Caffrey. He's back." I covered her shoulders in the thick white cream and started to rub it in.

"Liam who?"

"You know, from primary school." Our school was so big you could entirely lose people you didn't have classes with. "Thought he'd vanished off the face of the earth. Well, he's back and he's my new colleague."

"And?" Eden didn't look round.

"He's all right, y'know? I think you'd like him. He actually smiles when he hands the plates over, instead of just grunting."

"Sounds like *you* like him."

"Not like that. But it matters, the small stuff, when you've got a long shift."

"You haven't even started yet."

But I was looking forward to starting work in the café the next weekend. Now that Liam would be there. I tried to describe what made him different. "He talks to me like I'm . . ." Like what exactly? I chased down the words: "Like a person. Not a girl. Not a waitress. Not someone from his English class. Do you know what I mean?" I paused, nearly done with covering her back. I rubbed in a smear across her shoulder blades.

"Not a clue, J." Eden stretched out her arms, inspecting them. "Pass me the suntan lotion."

"Like I'm someone with options. Like he hasn't made up his mind about me yet." I passed the tube over. "Here."

"Well, you've only known him two minutes," she murmured, and I knew she wasn't really listening.

"Ten years. I'm just saying. There's not many lads like that. So comfy with who they are that they can handle whoever you are. You know?"

"Are you sure you don't fancy him?" She broke off from rubbing the cream into her arms and turned to grin at me.

"Nope. Missing the point, E . . . There! You're done. Chuck that tube over." I tapped her lightly and moved over to my chair to slather myself in the stuff. "No sunburn for us today."

"Ah, this is perfect." Eden settled down on her lounge chair with a long sigh.

"What the hell is this, then, delusional duo?" Iona's voice carried from inside the house, loud, clear, and drenched in sarcasm. She was beautiful, blond like Eden, but paler and more delicate. If you didn't know her, she seemed doll-like, all sweet and fragile, with those big blue eyes and a dusting of freckles across her nose.

Eden swore. "I knew this was too good to be true." She seemed to deflate a little, all her contentment leaking away.

Iona slouched through the open patio doors, wearing a vest and tight jeans, sunglasses on, carrying a pitcher in one hand, stacked glasses in the other. "Think you're in Beverly Hills? What a joke."

If her words were mean, it was her delivery that spiked them. Little word bombs exploding with hate.

"Mum made me bring you this: She thought you might need to cool down." Iona plonked the pitcher down on the metal table next to us, making the juice slop over the edge.

"So kind of you to think of us, dearest sister." Eden was sprawled, eyes closed, arms spread to catch the light.

"Then I'll be driving myself into town in a minute: music on, windows down." Iona had just passed her driver's test and loved reminding Eden of the fact. "So sorry you'll be stewing here . . . though I suppose you could always *walk* down later, once you've dried off." She reached into the pitcher and grabbed a handful of the ice cubes Claire had put in there.

"Eden . . . !" I warned, but Iona was too fast.

"Mum was right, you're definitely not cool enough." Iona smirked and slammed the ice cubes onto Eden's back before darting back inside.

"Argh!" Eden's shriek echoed down the valley. "Can't she give me a day off?" She sat up, furious, dripping. "Oof . . . Actually, it's quite nice. Definitely cooling. Probably even good for you, you know, like one of them spa treatments after a sauna. You should try it. . . ." She got a mischievous glint in her eye.

"Don't even go there!" But it was too late. She grabbed a handful of ice and chased me around the garden with it.

"Oi! Unprovoked!" Then of course I had to get revenge. By the time we'd finished, there was nothing left in the pitcher and we were sticky and damp and bent double, giggling.

"Right, there's only one thing for it. We need to swim."

"The dam? Hell, yeah. It'll be freezing. Let's do it!"

We grabbed our stuff and headed for the hill behind her house. I always forgot how hard the climb was. Just before the summit, surrounded by boulders and sheep poo, it felt like we'd never get there. Then suddenly, like a mirage, a flight of stone steps appeared ahead of us, looking as if they led up into the sky. . . .

"Race you!" We ran up them, laughing, and then there it was: a huge rectangular basin of water reflecting blue sky, built of stones, with a tiny golden beach in one corner. Our own local miracle, a beach on the high moors. And all around us in every direction, the view was amazing. Panoramic perfection, three hundred and sixty degrees.

Hot and sweaty, we dumped our things and waded in, flinching, on tiptoe, sucking our stomachs in against the cold.

"Flippin' freezing!" Eden yelped, then turned and watched me following.

I recognized the look in her eyes.

"Don't you dare splash me, Eden Holby." By August the water would be properly warm, heated by the stones all summer long, but it was hard to believe that now. "Oi! Two can do that, goose bump girl!" I splashed her back and we stumbled slowly forward in the soft sandy murk, till we were deep enough to plunge.

For the first few strokes, it felt as though we'd never be warm again. Gasping, we swam to the middle.

I pedaled my legs underwater, looking all around us, at the light on the water and the perfect unbroken blue above. I laughed, suddenly fizzy with happiness, dipped my head back and regretted it. The water was a vise around my skull, cold rising from the deeps at the dead center of the reservoir.

When I tilted back upright, Eden had a strange look on her face.

"E, what's up?" I asked her. "Don't tell me: You're peeing. *Ew!*"

She didn't even smile. "Jess, can I tell you something?"

"Course, E. What?" I nearly asked if we could go back to the beach first, but something in her face stopped me. We stayed right there.

I gave her time.

She bobbed down for a moment, then came up and spat out water. "Last night, I found something. I don't get it yet, but I think it's important. Promise me you won't tell anyone."

"Promise." I kept my eyes on her face, working my legs harder to keep my head steady above the water.

"Iona lost her passport, and she's got to get a new one really quick, before the holiday."

I nodded. Eden's dad was French and I knew they were off to see their gran in France at half-term, like always. "In three weeks, right?"

"Normally, Mum would make us fix it ourselves, something like that. Y'know, drag us all the way to the passport office to make a point, to teach us responsibility or something . . ."

"Yeah, mine's like that too. They can't help it—it's a mum thing."

"But this time she was very cagey. Wouldn't discuss it, just said she'd go herself." Eden was breathing harder now, using arms and legs to keep afloat. "And I know I shouldn't have done it, but Iona's been such a shit this week. When we're not at school, she's on me the whole time. I know she hates me, but it's worse lately."

"I know." I'd seen it too. Sometimes I caught the edge of Iona's hate, just from being with Eden. It hurt.

"So I wanted to see why Mum was being weird. I guess I wanted to use it against Iona." Her words came out choppy and breathless. "So I looked in Mum's desk, the locked one. I know where she keeps the keys. She's so obvious, with her totally guessable passwords, and her 'secret' keys hanging right next to the lock."

She stopped and clamped a hand over her mouth, making her sink a bit.

"What was it, E? What did you find?"

"Three passports. My birth certificate. And something else . . . Papers."

I could see it was serious. Her hair was wet, down her back, dark gold, streaky and shining in the sunshine. She was squinting against the light, and her eyes, that astonishing color, were like chips of blue glass, full of pain and something unfamiliar. She looked guilty.

She opened her mouth to tell me, but before she could speak, a bright yellow tennis ball slammed into the back of her head.

"What the f—?"

"Are you all right?" My hand shot out and grabbed her arm, holding her up, and we both spun round.

"Oi, what the hell? Who did that?" Eden's angry voice carried easily across the water, to the sloping wall of the reservoir where a handful of lads stood, guiltily, not looking our way.

Except one.

He raised his hand. "Me! So sorry. It was an accident. . . ." Liam Caffrey: the resurfaced mystery man, all grown up and gorgeous. Tall now, with that fair hair sticking up at the front. His face, all triangular with those killer cheekbones, and his dark eyebrows—telling you stuff his mouth hasn't said yet. I'd know him anywhere, even if I hadn't seen him yesterday.

But Eden wasn't listening. She grabbed the ball and tucked it under the wide front strap of her bikini, and then started hammering through the water toward him: front crawl, powered by fury, her elbows rising behind her and chopping through the water.

I bobbed after her more slowly, using my crap breaststroke, old lady–style, head above water.

Liam's mates started jeering and pointing. "You're in fer it now, mate!"

"Watch out for this one—that's Eden Holby."

Eden hauled herself to her feet, streaming water, and marched toward him, hardly slowed by the uneven rocks, chin jutting, pulling the ball out. "Your ball? How do you like it?" And she pulled her arm back and threw it straight at his head, from barely a foot away.

Liam didn't duck. He caught the ball, then froze, keeping it lifted. He was wearing just a pair of long baggy blue shorts, nothing else, and he didn't flinch in the face of her fury. His arm pulled back, like a loaded catapult.

"Good shot. Fair point. We quits now, or what?" His pale muscled chest rose and fell.

They stood there glaring at each other, head to head, without speaking.

Liam's mates waited, not daring to crack another joke till they saw which way it went.

Finally, Eden moved and pulled her glance away, scanning their stuff. "See them packets of salt and vinegar chips? Give me one. *Then* we're quits."

The tension broke up and rippled away to nothing. By the time I got out, Eden was sitting in the middle of the lads, passing a packet of chips around and laughing so hard at something Liam said that she sprayed herself with salty crumbs.

"Jess, where've you been? Hey, so I met the famous Liam Caffrey you've been telling me about. . . ."

"Hi, Jess, all right?" Liam's smile was bright and cloudless.

I smiled and waved and went to sit down with them, trying to work out why I felt as if something had been snatched away from me.

CHAPTER TEN

11:00 a.m.

"Eden and Liam. They got together in May. They were good for a bit, till June. Then, after Iona died . . ." I pause. It's hard putting it into words. "Well, it's like, me and Liam have been looking after Eden all summer."

The police officers write this down. I see Owl Lady notice Mum nodding along, backing me up.

"Do you get along with Liam?"

Flush. Burn. I nod, then lift my cup, taking scalding sips of tea so I don't have to meet their eyes.

"What's he like, Liam Caffrey?" Sleek Lady asks this one, casually.

I take a moment to consider all the different Liams, trying to bring them into one focused image.

Liam at work: steady, calm, capable. Him and the head chef, Dev, are a proper team, chopping, flipping, stirring, testing, building it all high and fancy on the plates like they do on the telly, and laughing at themselves for the effort.

Liam this summer: with me and Eden. Funny. Relaxed. Loving her so well, until . . . Liam at school: sullen, hunched, sweary. On a hair trigger: ready to erupt.

"He's sound. Really." It sounds pathetic, but how do you sum up anyone in just a few words?

"You know he attacked someone?" Sleek Lady gets her claws out. Meow.

"I heard he did something." I turn defensive. Liam was missing from school for weeks, and I never found out precisely which of the rumors were true. "But I bet he had a good reason. That Josh Clarkson is a nightmare."

"Jess!" Mum's shocked.

"So you're saying that you trust Liam Caffrey, despite his history?" Sleek Lady sounds as if she thinks that is an unwise thing to do.

"Totally." I ignore the irritating nag of suspicion tugging at my mind like a whiny kid. So what if Liam has a temper? So what if Liam hit someone? We all make mistakes. It doesn't mean anything.

Sleek Lady scribbles something, then smiles again and chucks in a hand grenade. "We know about the party last Saturday."

Tea. Gulping. "So?"

Mum's frowning. I know she wants me to cooperate.

"Tell us how Eden was last Saturday night. Who she spoke to. How she behaved."

I stall. The police did right by me last year. I didn't even have to enter the courtroom. Evidence by video link. A conviction. So I should do right by them now. But this isn't my story to tell. What if Eden's about to walk back in and I've told all her secrets to the police? But what if she's really in trouble and the police don't figure it out in time 'cause of something I hid?

"OK. There was a party. Mum, you know that—when her folks were called away to Eden's nan, the one who lives down south. They let her stay behind 'cause they didn't realize how poorly her grandma was. When they phoned to say they'd be away overnight, Eden took the chance to party. That's all! You can hardly blame her for wanting a good time, after everything she's been through!"

I know my tone's gone what Mum calls *belligerent*, but it is starting to feel like we're on trial here: me, Eden, Liam.

"Did Eden drink or take drugs?" Owl Lady asks casually.

Ouch.

"It's important that you tell us if she took anything on Saturday night. We're trying to build a picture of Eden's state of mind in the days leading up to her disappearance."

Her disappearance. I feel sick then. It's sinking in deeper. Every minute that passes, there is less chance of this script having a happy ending. This isn't a cliff-hanger episode of a soap after all. This might be a darker story, one of those crime shows after 9:00 p.m. This might not come out good.

Decision time. Truth or fudge?

I picture Eden: frightened, alone. Or worse: not alone.

"OK." I finish the sweet grainy dregs at the bottom of my mug and launch into the story of last weekend. Edited.

It was a long day in the café on Saturday for our last shift of the summer. Every time I dashed to the kitchen, Liam had some quip ready with the hot food.

"Here. Bean burgers for the vegans on table four. Beef burgers for the carnivores on table two. Or is it the other way round?" He grinned wickedly. "Bluff or double bluff? No tips for you if you're wrong."

"Give it a rest. I can tell the difference. You just watch me." I collected the plates, showing off with three up my arm, and sailed through the double doors.

My body felt tired from the work, but high with it too. I was buzzing from the dance of waitressing. I didn't mind the talking and the smiling. I didn't mind the heavy plates or the heat of the kitchen. I liked that it was straightforward. The tourists didn't know me. To them I was a function, not a freak. Best of all, it left no time to think.

When we'd finished, Liam emerged from the kitchen, flushed from the heat. I passed over his share of the coins I'd been counting. "Record tips. You can thank me later."

"Ah, Jess. You rock. Nice work."

"What can I say? We're a good team."

His smile was the best reward, but I made myself look away and grab my phone. "Come on, Eden's texted. She'll be wondering where we've got to."

We went out into the sunshine to find Eden in the park.

"Three-day weekend starts here," I said, stealing a glance up at Liam's face. We had a bank holiday on Monday. He reminded me of a cat or a fox: something sleek, with hidden teeth. Yes, a fox, that was it, with those slanting cheekbones, angled toward me.

He'd changed—jeans and a faded red T-shirt—with his chef's whites in his backpack to wash. I'd switched my work shirt for my favorite tee. Now I shook my hair down and put my studs back in.

"Yep. Don't even think about Tuesday. Deal?" He offered me his fist. His eyebrows were telling me it was time to play.

"Deal." I tapped his knuckles with mine, and it didn't even cause a ripple. Maybe I was getting better.

I crossed the street with Liam. It felt good, being by his side. We sank into being off duty, like sliding into a deep bath. It was one of those long hot summer Saturdays when the concrete soaked up the heat and served it back to you at dusk like a bonus. Sergei in the ice-cream van still had a long queue. That idiot Jack Greenwood from Year Eight had just dive-bombed into the canal in his jeans, his stupid little mates cheering. We dodged aimless tourists, still drifting like clouds of midges around the park gates.

Eden was perched on the back of a bench at the edge of the skate park where it met the kids' playground. The dividing line was one thin red railing. Eden was picking idly at the peeling paint, flicking off the dry flakes like giant scabs. She saw us and uncurled herself slowly, then came over to hug us both in turn, Liam first. She was wearing cutoff denim shorts that my mum would say were too short and a blue daisy-print vest, bloodred lipstick, and black sunglasses. She looked stunning.

I ran one hand over my face and hair, feeling suddenly greasy and stale from the café. I followed Eden's gaze. She was watching some strangers through the iron bars.

"What's up?" I asked.

"Losers." Liam dismissed them.

The lads were about our age, a handful of them, but not from around here. They were sitting in the playground before all the little kids and parents left for the night. They'd brought loud music and cans of beer in plastic bags, and they were skinning up at a picnic table with no effort to hide it.

You didn't do that. Not in a town this small. The news would get home before I did.

"Good day at work, dears?" Eden turned her attention back to us, her voice sneering and sarcastic.

My heart sank. You never knew which Eden you were going to get, since Iona. Mum sat me down and explained it, so I knew it was normal, that grief meant anger and denial.

I braced myself, shields up. "Yeah, not bad. Bit busy. Good tips at least."

Liam laughed at that. Private joke.

I smiled back at him, but Eden jumped in quickly, taking control again. "Finally, your last shift! You're all mine now!" Her voice had an edge that made me wonder how much she'd minded us working together, without her. "Free till school on Tuesday."

"Shh. No one mention the *S*-word. Me and Jess already struck that deal." Liam stretched out on the bench, all long limbs and broad shoulders.

I sat awkwardly apart on one side, while Eden threw herself down on the other and cozied into Liam's chest.

"I'm in. We're free! *Free-eee . . . to feel good!*" she sang, from an old song they'd been playing in the café that summer. "Come on—let's do something. It's our last Saturday of freedom. And guess what—my parents aren't coming home tonight after all."

I sat up and looked at them. Liam rolled his eyes in my direction, eyebrows raised in alert: not unkind, just putting us both on standby. We'd had to develop a kind of shorthand for looking after Eden this summer. It was clearly going to be one of *those* days.

Eden jumped up. She started climbing over the iron railings, ignoring their pointed tips.

"Bloody hell, Eden, can't you just go around like a normal person?" But he vaulted after her, one-handed, making it look easy.

I sighed and took the long way round, which didn't involve gymnastics. When I walked through the gates, Eden was in the center of the new gang. They circled her, fascinated. She flipped her hair over her shoulder, delivering a punch line that made them all laugh.

I smothered a flare of anger, wondering whether I should just walk away now and head home. New people made me edgy. Eden knew that, but this summer she was selfish. With good reason. I hated myself for even thinking it.

I looked at the strangers more closely. The leader seemed to be a tall lad, very cool in his designer vest, baggy shorts, and gold jewelry standing out against his black skin. He had the added glamour of being new—plus, huge brown eyes and a wide, white smile—and I watched Eden home in on that, laughing and flirting on full beam.

She was ignoring Liam, who waited at the edge like a restless golden Labrador.

"Hey, this is Tyler. He's just moved here," she called out to us. "Tyler, meet Liam 'n' Jess." The way she said it made it sound like we were a unit, and I wondered if she'd done that on purpose, to free her up.

"Hi," I muttered, keeping a wary distance.

Liam nodded without speaking.

"So, *E-den*,"—Tyler said it slowly, as if it tasted sweet—"what is there to do after dark in this little town?"

I snorted. See how she coped with that one. There were old men's pubs, a gay women's bar, the one club.

"All back to mine?" Eden offered. "Folks are away. Eden will play. Liam can bring the tunes," she sang.

"A party? For me? We only just met. I heard you northern girls ain't shy." Tyler was pushing his luck. His mates laughed, egging him on. "We won't say no, will we, lads?"

Liam stepped closer. "It's not for you, it's for Eden," he growled.

Eden preened, delighted by the tension, looking from Liam to Tyler and back again.

"*Eden, no!*" I didn't like it. I hated this mood. It was one thing with me or Liam, pushing us, winding us up, to distract her from the darkness in her own head, but not with strangers. They wouldn't know to be careful with her.

"You got that wrong, Jess," she taunted me. "You mean: *Eden, yes*. Today, Eden only says yes." Her eyes held Tyler's, dancing with mischief.

She was too far gone to think of me. To remember that I'm not good with big groups or strangers, and why . . .

"*Yes* sounds good. A party sounds better. Here, to get you started." Tyler leaned in close to Eden as he passed over something hidden inside his cupped hand.

I knew she didn't usually smoke, but she wasn't going to drop the banter this far into the game. "Yes. Why not?" She narrowed her eyes and blew out smoke—I inhaled the sweet, rich, herbal scent of skunk. There'd be no stopping her now.

I bit my lip. I had to be careful how I played it. If I pushed it and she barred me, I couldn't look out for her.

Liam scowled but stayed silent. I wondered if he was having the same battle.

"Whatever." I shrugged, decision made. For Eden's sake, I was in. I was on board for whatever crazy night she had planned. "When are they back? Monday? Got two days to clean up . . ." I kept my tone as light as hers, not passing judgment.

She got her phone out and her thumb flitted over its surface. She pressed hard, one last time, and looked up, grinning. "Done. It's live. Don't worry, I invited you, Jess. Liam, you get the lead slot on the decks. Now help me out, will you? We've got an hour and a half to prepare the party of our lives."

CHAPTER ELEVEN

And she did it too. We got a taxi up to Eden's place, leaving the others to follow on later, calling at Liam's for the decks and speakers, scooping up his mate Aziz along the way.

"Where're your mum and dad?" I asked as we barged in, carrying boxes of records—these boys favored vinyl. The house was very quiet, but it didn't stay that way for long. Liam and Az followed on our heels, lugging a massive speaker between them.

"Nan's been taken ill again. She's in hospital."

"Really sorry, E."

Eden blanked the sympathy. No change there.

"I got a pass out, long as I eat dinner with Mrs. Coates next door. But I just texted her to say I can't make it."

"She'll hear the music," I pointed out.

"Yeah, but you know what? I'm still playing the dead-sister card. Gets me out of all kinds of crap. Come on!"

I felt a gathering sense of dread, storm clouds rolling in. This wasn't right. Eden wasn't right. I knew she loved her nan.

Could the real Eden Holby please come back? It seemed like only a faint possibility.

I joined Eden in her manic party prep, while Liam and Az set up the music. To be fair, Eden managed to lock most of the stuff worth stealing in her dad's office. Then we pushed back the furniture in the huge living room, hiding it beneath old bedsheets, and moved the table and chairs in the dining room opposite.

Liam set up his DJ booth in the hall that joined them, and this became the dance floor, spilling off left to right into each room.

We filled the sink with ice, and Eden packed it with bottles of beer and liquor stolen from the cellar. She found a ball of string in one of the kitchen drawers and tied it across the wide staircase like a giant spiderweb to stop people from exploring upstairs.

"See! All thought through. It's going to be fine," she told me triumphantly. Her eyes were already glassy, her pupils massive and inky. "Now our turn!" she pulled me up the staircase and we had to crawl under the string web, giggling.

"You know the only good thing about having a dead sister?" Eden called over her shoulder, once we were through.

I flinched at her words.

"Two wardrobes are better than one!" She marched into Iona's room. I leaned on the doorframe, watching as she flung Iona's wardrobe doors wide and started flicking through her stuff.

I remembered Iona's room had always been tidy, but now it was a museum piece, frozen in time. It gave me a weird feeling, seeing all her stuff waiting for her—her posters and photos pinned up on the walls, her hairbrush and bottles of nail varnish on the window ledge, her necklaces and scarves draped over the mirror, the bright red throw and cushions on her bed. I glanced behind me into the corridor, half expecting her to come charging in, cursing us.

Iona wasn't coming. She was never coming back to her room. The finality of it made the four walls spin around me. "Eden, you sure 'bout this?" I asked, rubbing a sweaty palm across my forehead.

"Yeah, course. What's she going to do? Haunt me?" She kept on flicking through the hangers without turning round. "I should tell the world, shouldn't I? Tell them I've got proof that ghosts don't exist. You can bet your last fiver—if she could, Iona would haunt me twenty-four-seven!"

When had this happened? It was as if Eden's grief had been pushed down, under the pressure of everything unresolved, and it had changed into something hard and cold, deep down inside her.

I imagined this unbreakable core, spreading out inside Eden—like a story from one of those old Marvel comics—replacing her flesh and bones till she wasn't human anymore, she was Titanium Girl, hard and brittle and cruel.

"You know what?" She pulled out a black jumpsuit and held it against her, looking in the mirrored door. "She's been my age plus two all our lives. Not anymore. Her clock stopped ticking at seventeen. So I'm going to catch up. Soon I will overtake her. Now *I* get to be the oldest. She'd bloody hate that, if she knew. . . ."

"Eden." I moved toward her, wanting to stop this stream of bitterness.

"This!" Eden spun round, triumphant, holding up a black dress on a hanger. She talked fast, not letting me get a word in edgeways. "Come on, Jess. Not long now. Let's get changed."

I was glad to leave Iona's room. We went next door into Eden's. It had those little old-fashioned windows built under the eaves and I could see out, across the wide sunlit valley. The sunset caught the distant windows of the houses opposite, tiny squares of burning gold.

Eden put on the radio and started singing as she stripped down to her underwear. "Hurry up, Jess, people will be here soon. You can't wear that old thing. Borrow whatever you like. . . ."

We didn't usually do this: Our styles and sizes were too different. It felt weird, pawing through her things, as if wearing Eden's clothes might turn me into her. Once, not so long ago, I'd've jumped at the chance. Right now, it wasn't somewhere I wanted to go. Being Eden looked complicated and painful. Right now, I'd honestly rather be me, and that was saying something.

However, I did as I was told. I settled for a red lace top I hadn't seen her wear in months. It came down over my hips, but it would do.

"There! Perfect, J!" Eden took my shoulders and turned me to the mirror.

She looked amazing, as usual. Iona's dress was short and tight, making her long tanned legs look endless. She'd retouched her makeup and done her hair with tongs so it tumbled down her back in thick curls. It was Iona's red lipstick, and Iona's style.

If any of Iona's friends turned up, they'd get a shock. Maybe that was the point: Eden was being the bad sister now that the job was vacant.

And me? Even I looked all right. I lined my eyes, thick and black, taking dark shadow right up to the brow. I painted my lips a deeper shade than Eden's. The red top matched my hair and made it glow.

"Red suits you, J. You look fab."

I spoke into the mirror, watching our faces, taking a deep breath and daring to conjure up some honesty: "You don't have to do this. You can change your mind, take down the invite."

"And why would I want to do that?" she asked, turning icy.

That trick never worked on me. "E, listen up: I'm worried about you." I dropped the pretense of keeping cool. I turned and looked up at the real Eden, not the reflection of a girl dressed up as someone else because being herself hurt too much right now. "Where's it going to stop, E? When are you gonna stop running?" I looked into her dark-blue eyes and said, "You know I've got your back, but maybe you should slow down and admit—"

"Lighten up, Jess." She interrupted me in a voice that was hoarse with something close to tears. "Don't do this now, I mean it. . . ."

Just then the music started downstairs, so loud it made the window frames vibrate.

Eden's laughter was high-pitched hysteria. "Here we go!" She spun away from me, running down the corridor.

I followed more slowly, ducking under that stupid string. I felt self-conscious on the grand staircase, like I was making a Cinderella-style entrance, even though there were only four of us in the house.

Az looked up from fiddling with an extension lead, saw me, and whistled.

Liam, flicking through a box of records, glanced up and paused. His expression changed, just for a moment. The next look that blew across his face was the usual one, warm and friendly, but I'd seen something else for a split second and I held it in my heart, a tiny glimmer of hope and fear, as fragile and dangerous as a real spark.

An hour later, cars were jamming the lane outside. By the time Tyler and his mates arrived, things were definitely out of hand. Strangers were arriving from Manchester. Some lad I didn't know was puking in a flower bed. The bodies were so tightly packed on the dance floor that Ed Foster from the year above me started crowd surfing between rooms. Az yelled at a tall dark-haired lad in a Burnley football club shirt for sliding down the banister and making the decks shake on the dismount. By midnight, the lights were out. Eden was dancing over candles on the dining table in perfectly coordinated underwear, while Liam played her favorite tunes. Tyler was right there, drinking it all in. In the flickering light, his eyes were huge dark pools, never straying from Eden.

I just hid. I found a spot near the door, a kind of alcove with a window seat behind a creamy-gold curtain, where I felt safe, where I could keep an eye on Eden. I had a tall glass of whiskey and Coke for company. I stayed behind my curtain, watching, watching, watching. My drink warmed me up. I leaned my head on the open window and took deep breaths of night air when the shakes got too bad: my breath misting the glass and then fading.

When I was calmer, I looked back inside and watched it like a reality TV show. I watched Tyler pass Eden something small, round, and pale. I watched Eden tip her head back and swallow it. I watched how she took Tyler's drink—a shot of gold liquid— and then kissed him on the lips. I watched Tyler follow Eden upstairs, ducking under the string barrier.

My eyes found Liam. His hands were clenched fists, frozen above the decks. The track wanted mixing, and he messed it up. The house fell into sudden silence. People started heckling.

"Hey, mate, if it was my turn, you only needed to holler." Az nudged Liam over. "Come on, man, you're making me look bad." He flicked the fader up and the room erupted again: hands in the air, people yelling along.

I was the only one watching Liam lose it. Behind Az, Liam punched his fist into the wall. His face was transformed into a Halloween mask of jealousy and rage. Jekyll into Hyde, or was it the other way around?

I managed to crush my fear so small that I could cross the sea of people dancing. I even managed not to scream when they slammed up against me, with their hands and their shoulders and the warm weight of their bodies. I managed to reach Liam. I managed to touch his arm.

But I must have been white and shaking, 'cause he only had to look at me once. Then it was Liam leading me outside into the cool night air and down the garden path.

CHAPTER TWELVE

11:18 a.m.

I edit this into a brief account for adult consumption and serve it up to the police and my mum.

"OK, so I'm going to assume Eden drank alcohol, may have taken Class A drugs, and probably didn't get much sleep." Owl Lady police officer sums it up neatly. "Jess, I'm not judging. We're looking at risk factors. We're looking at people. We're building a picture, as I said."

I feel like an informer. I take another gulp of sweet tea— Mum must have refilled my mug without me noticing.

"Did you go back inside after that?"

I shake my head.

"Sunday? What happened then?"

"She slept is what happened," Mum puts in. "Personal best: one fifteen in the afternoon. Then she went running. Nothing to report." She sounds defensive. I'm grateful someone else is speaking for a change.

"Did you talk to Eden?"

I shake my head. "We texted. Plans for Monday, a shopping trip. I think Tyler was with her Sunday, maybe." I skirt around the stuff I can't mention. "I did my longest run, watched TV, nothing much." I shrugged. I'd run all the way up to Stoodley Pike—that old monument stuck like a needle into the highest, flattest point of the moor—and by the time I got back, my hangover was gone.

Sleek Lady takes over. "Right, so much for Sunday. Then you spent bank holiday Monday with Eden? Where did you go? Was she herself, would you say?"

. • ⦂ • •

It was a good thing I'd run so far or I couldn't have slept on Sunday night. As it was, I woke at six and lay there worrying for hours, going over the events of Saturday night. How I would raise it with her. *So, about Saturday night. You were off with Tyler, so I'm guessing you won't mind I spent most of the party with Liam.*

When the text from Eden came through—*Station at 11?*— it was a relief and a deadline all at once. By 11:10, I'd know how she was and what she knew.

It didn't work like that. She was late, of course. I got the tickets and stood outside the station, feeling sick with dread. The weather seemed to understand. It was gray, not even wet, just damp and still, as if we were all suspended in a cloud.

The Leeds train pulled in. People got off and filed out of the station past me. Then, at the last possible moment, Eden appeared in a taxi. She tumbled out, calling over her shoulder, and we just had time to run for it before the train doors hissed behind us and the guard muttered something grumpily about cutting it close.

My heart felt like it might jump right out of my chest. I wondered about hiding in the loo, but they always smelled so bad I'd be guaranteed to throw up. The only two free seats were at a table, and we flopped into them opposite two women plugged into their phones.

I hid my panic by babbling on about the train tickets and passing Eden's over to her with sweaty fingers.

I glanced at her sideways. What did she know? What had Liam said? Was she waiting for the right moment to bring it up?

Eden settled back and stared out of the window. She did look like crap: chalky beneath her tan, with massive purple-blue shadows under her eyes that the most expensive concealer in the world couldn't hide. Had she been crying? I remembered the pill she'd taken. I was no expert, but I'd heard that a comedown could feel like flu.

"You OK?" I asked, hating myself. I was a hypocrite. "House get cleared all right?"

She shrugged. "Found a website. Be good as new when I get back."

That was the thing about being rich. It could fix the small stuff. In the unlikely event I ever threw a party, no doubt I'd spend the next two days on my hands and knees scrubbing away the puke.

She didn't mention Saturday night again and neither did I. We compared shopping lists. Polite. Subdued. I could feel the presence of everything we didn't say. It felt like some invisible creature sitting between us—like one of the story lines from *Doctor Who*. This monster would grow bigger and bigger the more we ignored it, till finally it would destroy us both. We talked like strangers, every bland word I said sticking in my throat, and all the while the little silent monster grew, guzzling away on my guilt and paranoia.

In Leeds, I trailed after Eden in near-silence as she went around her favorite shops, buying ankle boots, a jacket, tinted lip gloss, same as the last. Then she humored me in Paperchase—she knew I loved that shop. But even color-coordinated piles of stationery couldn't cheer me up today. I only got two sketch-books, three pens, and a new pad of sticky notes.

Instead of lunch, she bought us overpriced coffees laden with sweet syrup and frothy milk. As we were finishing the dregs, I couldn't bear it anymore. I watched my best friend looking miserable, and I'd had enough. I'd just blurt it all out, beg for her forgiveness, and then at least this waiting would be over. I felt like I was on death row.

"Can we talk?" I asked, looking down at my knotted fingers, palms suddenly damp. I dared one quick glance.

"Yeah. Course." She looked surprised. "But can we do it on the train back? Just, it's time. We have to go now or I'll be late." She picked up her phone and stood up, expectantly.

"Late for what?"

She flicked her eyes at me, but said only, "Come on."

I shrugged and stood up, feeling my heart slowing again: confrontation postponed.

She used the app on her phone to navigate through the city center, walking fast, taking sudden turns, leaving the main shopping zone. Finally we ducked into a cobbled alleyway and she stopped so abruptly that I crashed into the sheaf of oversize boutique bags she'd slung on her left wrist.

"Number 54 . . ." she mumbled, peering up.

"What is it, E? What are we doing here?" In my sleep-deprived state, the day had taken on an eerie, dreamlike feel. I had no idea what we were doing. Why wouldn't Eden tell me anything? It wasn't my paranoia: Eden was definitely being weird, and the day seemed to reflect her strangeness.

We were standing outside a dingy arcade in an old Victorian building that had seen better times. Sure enough, the number 54 was worked into the fancy stained glass above the double doors. The ornate metalwork had once been white and was now stained with specks of rust like dried blood.

"Will you stay with me?" Eden asked, one hand on the door. She looked at me through half-closed eyes. In the dimness of the doorway she was deathly pale.

I bit down more questions. "Course I will, E. Always." I felt a rush of protectiveness for her, so warm and strong that I could forget for a whole minute what I'd done.

We went inside. It couldn't have been more different from the sleek gold-and-glass arcade of designer boutiques up the road. This place was shabby and half the shops were boarded up. There was a secondhand clothes shop, a vinyl record store, and a shopfront full of dog-eared posters listing the benefits of Traditional Chinese Medicine. My attention was snagged by a graphic-novel and comics store displaying some new Japanese imports.

But Eden was already heading up a wooden staircase in the center of the building, the kind that folded around one of those elevator shafts, like you see in old films, with the cables and all that mechanical stuff I'd rather not think about when I get in an elevator.

The upper floor was even quieter, echoey and full of shadows. It smelled damp and cold. The dreamlike atmosphere deepened.

"Where are we going?" I asked. "Are you sure this is right? It doesn't look—"

"Here."

To our left, a sign announced THE ANGEL'S GIFT, framed with gaudy red-and-black gothic artwork that put my teeth right on edge. In the window, there were ornaments, clusters of crystals, candles, and other things I couldn't name.

"This is it," Eden said, putting her phone away. She pushed the glass door open and a loud clang of wind chimes signaled our arrival.

"Welcome, welcome!" A middle-aged woman rose from a stool behind the till to greet us, beaming.

I stared, baffled. This was so not Eden's kind of place. It smelled sweet and faintly smoky.

The woman wore a green dress under a long brown woolly vest thing. She had frizzy gray hair escaping from a bun, and her eyes twinkled at us over little half-moon glasses. "What can I help you with, dears?"

She suited the rest of the shop so perfectly that it was hard not to snicker.

"I'm here for a reading," Eden replied.

A *reading*? I looked for evidence of books and found a few. Not the kind Eden read.

"Ellie Caffrey. Three o'clock."

I searched Eden's face. She wouldn't meet my eye. Stung, I muttered under my breath, "Nice false name, E."

The woman opened a large scheduling book and ran a finger down to the appointment, ticking it off in green ink.

"What?" I whispered to Eden. "What the hell's going on?" I nudged her, trying to break the spell and reenter reality.

But Eden didn't reply, all still and stiff and pale next to me.

"Just settle up with me first, dear, and then you're free to focus. Thirty pounds, please."

Eden handed over the crumpled notes. The woman took the money and fumbled for change. She froze with her hand in midair as a thought occurred to her. "You did say you were over eighteen, dear?"

"Of course," Eden snapped, taking the tenner.

Liar. Like when I got my tattoo—just how far will the truth stretch for us?

"Right. You're just through the red curtain at the back, with Debs. I'll put the kettle on for after, all right? Good luck, dear." Frizzy Lady seemed undisturbed by Eden's rudeness.

We walked hesitantly over to the other side of the shop, circling around a display cabinet labeled BIRTHSTONE JEWELRY.

"What? Here?" Eden pointed, and Frizzy Lady nodded vigorously. Eden pulled the curtain back and we entered a different space.

There was a huge round window on the exterior wall, flooding the little cubbyhole with greenish-gray light filtered through the old glass. We could be underwater, looking out through a porthole at submerged city streets.

"What is this?" I tried again gently. "Why are we here?"

She didn't answer, scanning the room with wide eyes.

It was neat and clean in there, with a round wooden table and four matching chairs. There were some lilies on the shelf in a gold pot, and a stack of blue glasses and a blue water pitcher. It seemed more like the expensive salon where Eden had her hair cut, and I felt her relax, just a little.

"Hi there." A younger woman appeared from behind another curtain and came to sit facing us. "I'm Debs Green. Welcome."

We stared.

She smiled. "I know, I get that a lot. Don't tell me: I don't look like a tarot reader. You expected someone like Irene out there, didn't you?"

Tarot? Eden? Now I was sure I was dreaming. Eden didn't go for that stuff. She always said, *If you can't taste it, it's not real.*

Debs wore a tight-fitting wraparound dress in a spiraling blue print. She was in her thirties, I guessed, with long, glossy, honey-colored hair in a low ponytail. She wore a necklace of interlocking gold rings and her smile was very white and shiny. If you'd made me guess, I'd pin her as a dental nurse on a night out.

"Which of you is Ellie?" Debs asked.

Eden jumped at the fake name, a beat too late. "Me. I am."

"Take a seat. Do you want your friend to stay? Or wait out there with Irene?"

"Stay. Please." Eden gave me a pleading look and I saw that she was scared.

"Sit down, both of you." She gestured at the chairs. "Would you like a drink of water?"

We shook our heads, sitting on the edge of the seats. Neither of us took our coats off. Eden was gripping the handles of her shopping bags so tightly that her knuckles were white.

"So. There are a few ways we could approach this, Ellie," Debs began. "Would you like to tell me something of what's on your mind? The question that brings you today?"

I stared at Eden, willing her to meet my eyes, to give me something here. What the hell was she playing at? Was this an elaborate way to catch me out?

Eden's eyes remained firmly on Debs. "Do I have to?"

"No. OK. That's fine. You don't have to." Her smile faded as she fixed her gaze on Eden. The atmosphere in the room changed. Debs examined her intently, like she was listening to something no one else could hear. Was this part of the act?

Eden gazed back. Her cheeks flushed slightly, but she didn't break eye contact.

Debs reached for an ornate box on the shelf and took out a stack of cards. There were about as many as in a pack of playing cards, but these were larger.

"Take the deck, Ellie. Give it a shuffle, OK?"

Eden nodded, and when she reached for them, I noticed her fingers were trembling.

"Have you had your cards read before?"

Headshake.

When someone once brought a tarot deck into school and everyone crowded around, Eden was the one who'd laughed and walked away. But that was the old Eden, the one from before.

"When you see the cards, try not to judge them, OK? Some of the images can be pretty dramatic, but the meanings are more subtle. You need to let me interpret them, OK?" Her smile was warm and reassuring. "That's what you've paid me for, isn't it?"

Eden fumbled and dropped a card.

I started to feel too hot in the enclosed space. I wished I'd never followed Eden here. It came to me in a sudden rush what a mistake I'd made. What if the cards told her about me? What if it was all about betrayal? The Traitor? Was that even a card?

My breathing came fast and shallow as I watched Eden struggle to shuffle the pack.

"Is that enough?" Eden whispered.

"Sure. When you're ready, put the pack down. Then cut it three times." Debs demonstrated the movement in the air, her manicured fingernails glinting palely in the watery light.

"As you prefer to keep your intentions private—and that's fine, I respect that—I'm going to start with a very short reading, OK? Just three cards, symbolizing the past, present, and future, with reference to your question. Then I'll read them for you."

What was Eden really here for? The mention of the past sent me spiraling. My past. Eden's past. There were shadows there.

Eden nodded. A hand flew up and played with a loose bit of hair around her face. Then she leaned over to cut the cards. One stuck to her fingers and she had to shake it off.

Finally the pack just sat there. We looked at it, as if we expected it to start doing tricks all on its own.

Then Debs slid the top three cards onto the smooth wooden tabletop and turned them over one by one.

The first card read DEATH and had a medieval-looking illustration of a grim reaper.

Shit. As if Eden needed a reminder.

The second had a load of swords stabbing into a bleeding heart, and the number 9.

I glared at Debs. What was she trying to do?

The third was a bright gold star, like a kid's drawing.

Eden choked out, "No!" She stood up so fast that her chair toppled back with a loud crash. She grabbed her bags and pushed through the curtains. I heard the door chimes jangle and the sound of feet running down the stairs outside.

"Ellie, wait!"

"I-I-I need to go after her. Sorry!" I blurted, halfway out of my chair too.

"Wait." Debs was fierce suddenly. "Listen to me. This is important. She needs to know what the cards mean. It's not what she thinks."

Something in her eyes made me sit back down to listen.

"Ellie's having a tough time, I can see that. Please? Promise me you'll tell her this?"

"Yeah, sure, whatever, I promise."

She spoke urgently, seeing I was itching to be out of there.

"The death card doesn't mean death. It can be change, endings, but it's really a kind of rebirth, OK? This one, the nine of swords: That's where she is now, and she's suffering. She's in pain. But look, the star here? That's her future and it means healing, see? So tell her, these cards are not bad. They are positive. They show that there's hope ahead."

I flick my eyes over the cards again, trying to memorize them. "OK, so it's change, suffering now, hope ahead. Got it, thanks. I have to run."

The arcade was empty. And the alleyway beyond. I ran as fast as I could back toward the station, getting snarled in the bank-holiday crowds. I was scanning at every step, left to right, up the streets and down them, searching for Eden's denim jacket, for a flash of long blond hair.

The anxiety built as I retraced our steps, faster, faster, faster. I looked for her everywhere. I grew frantic. I made people tut and stare as I pushed past them. Three times I rang her phone. Three times it went straight to voice mail. I started sprinting.

I hurried through the turnstile at Leeds station, and stood under the announcement screens, bouncing with impatience till I found the right train.

"Shit! Platform 11B." I had less than a minute. Sure enough, I looked across the tracks to my left and saw the train pulling slowly away.

My phone buzzed in my hand.

Sorry. Need time on my own. See you at school in morning.
E xxx

I went up the escalator in a daze and found a seat at the top, by the coffee kiosk. I tapped out a long message to Eden, telling her everything Debs had said about the cards. Then I sat there staring into space, feeling more tired than I'd ever felt in my life, while the coffee machine gasped and shrieked in my ear.

How could I have thought she was getting better? Yes, she put on a good act, but I should've seen through it. Seen through her swagger on Saturday. Seen the truth: that she was desperate enough to seek out stuff she'd never normally touch. If Eden was ready to pay for a tarot reading, I prayed she'd believe in the cards' message of hope. But a familiar niggling fear was back, and it started growing in the darkest corner of my mind.

CHAPTER THIRTEEN

11:36 a.m.

I finish telling the police officers about the tarot cards. Out of the corner of my eye I can sense Mum about to explode at me for not mentioning this before.

"I know it all sounds bad, today . . . but I didn't know . . ." I sound like I'm pleading innocence, even though I know I'm guilty. If anyone should have seen this coming, it's me. "Yes, I've been worried about her this summer. But it's not been all bad. She's been up and down. But she seemed OK at school this week . . . ," I conclude lamely. "I thought we were getting back to normal."

They've been making notes all along without interrupting. Now, Owl Lady quizzes me about Tyler.

"What's his surname?"

"I don't know."

"Where does he live?"

I shrug. "He said he'd just moved here. Shouldn't be too hard to find."

"Has Eden been in touch with him?"

"Sunday, he was there, I think. Dunno since then."

Eyebrows.

"Look, they only met on Saturday. They got together that night. She's barely mentioned him since." And come to think of it, that should've set alarm bells ringing. We usually talked all the angles. If she wasn't discussing Tyler, did that mean it *was* serious? Serious on a whole new level? I chase that thought down some dark alleyways.

"How did Liam react to Tyler? Was he angry with him? Or with Eden?"

"No!" It comes out too loud and they're right on it. "I mean, he was frustrated; who wouldn't be?" I'm trying so hard to sound reasonable that I hardly recognize my own voice. "But Liam barely spoke to Tyler. And like I said, this week's been close to normal. She said she was meeting Liam last night."

"So you don't think he resented Eden for choosing Tyler on Saturday?"

The truth burns like an ember in my mouth, but I'm not letting it out: It could spark off a whole new blaze. I swallow it. "We've been there for Eden, all summer, whatever she did." That's my version of "no comment." I see her write something down on her notepad, angled away so I can't read it.

"How was Liam this week?"

"I don't know." I hate to admit it. "I haven't really spoken to him since Saturday night."

More writing in the notebook.

More heat in my cheeks.

"Where do you think Eden is?" Owl Lady takes a new angle, and her focus has changed, gone steely. "Did she have a favorite place? Somewhere she might be?"

"I don't *know!*" For the first time, I raise my voice. "I've told you *everything.*" Apart from minor incriminating details that don't affect their search, because Eden will always be my priority. Before she can hit back with the next question, I get in there first. "So what are you going to do? What's next? Where are you going to look for her now?"

"Our colleagues have conducted a first search of the premises and the immediate vicinity. Other options will be explored as the investigation progresses."

Premises. Vicinity. Progresses. I hate her careful neutral language. She means Eden's home. She means around here. She means if Eden doesn't turn up. I can feel my breathing speeding up. I clutch my warm empty mug so hard that I think it might shatter.

"I can assure you, we'll do everything in our power to ensure Eden is found as soon as possible. The investigatory team is highly experienced."

How can they be? It's not as if this happens every week around here. But I don't say that. A plan starts forming in my head. Their questions have shown me the way. There *are* places Eden could be. There's a whole load of them: all our favorite ones, from the dam to the waterfall and everywhere in between.

The police might have paperwork and procedure, but I don't. I'm free, or I soon can be. And I'm fast. I've been training for a half marathon. I can cover miles in a day. I'm going to do what they won't do. I'm going to get out there and retrace all our steps this summer. I've given the police the information, but I can't wait for them to act on it. The investigation might not crank up for days. I need to act now.

Sleek Lady is saying, "Can I confirm your mobile number?"

Confirm? That means they have it already. I reel it off, obediently.

"We'll be in touch if we have any further questions. And if you hear from Eden, we need you to let us know immediately."

They gather their notes.

"Thank you, Jess." Owl Lady is the senior one, wrapping things up now: "I know it can't be easy, talking to us today."

I look at her sharply. Does she mean because of my history? Or because of Eden's?

"Now the best you can do is get back to school. If Eden rings you, or if you think of anything else that might help the investigation, however small, call me at this number." She passes me a card with the West Yorkshire Police logo and her number and email printed on it.

I take it, embarrassed that my fingers are damp and trembling.

They stand. "Thank you for the tea. And your time, Jess, and you, Ms. Mayfield."

I manage to mutter good-bye as Mum shows them out.

When Mum comes back in, she seems smaller somehow. "I can't believe I'm saying this, but why don't you take the rest of the day off, Jess? I don't care what the police said. I want you here, safe, under my roof, till all this is over." She sits back down on the chair next to me and grabs my hand tightly.

Not this again. I thought we were past the overprotective insanity.

"I mean, what if there's someone out there who's hurt Eden? What if they hurt you too?" Her voice starts wobbling. "I can't let that happen again, Jess. I will not. Do you hear me?"

"Mum. Stop it!" I shout to jolt her out of this reaction, and pull my hand back. "It's not the same. We don't know if someone's hurt Eden. But I know she's out there somewhere." I brace myself to tell her my plan. "I'm going to go and find her. I have to bring her back."

"Jess, no!" She is as shocked as if I've slapped her. She grabs my wrists, as though she's going to physically keep me here. "No! I won't let you."

"Mum!" She can't mean this. "Do you really think I can sit inside and do nothing? *Mum!*"

She looks at me, and I can see that's exactly what she wants. For me to be safe at any cost.

"Mum, no." I try to get through to her coaching brain, the bit that's not in maternal meltdown. "I have to do this. Don't you see?" I take a breath and say the worst thing I've thought today so far, no matter how much it hurts me to say the words: "And if it all goes wrong . . ."—*If Eden is dead*, I mean—"at least I'll know I tried. I didn't hide, or sit it out. I got out there and did everything in my control. *Please?*"

I don't care if I'm begging her. I need to get out there and *do* something.

She lets go of my arms, and I can see there's a battle raging inside her.

Tick, tick, tick . . .

"Jess, I'm sorry, but no." That's her final voice. Her serious don't-mess-with-me voice. The big guns. It usually works 'cause she doesn't bring it out much. "I've made my decision. You can't just wander around alone, hoping you stumble upon Eden. Leave it to the police. They're the professionals. You can do some homework here today. You are not going out there till we know Eden's safe. Or . . ." She changes tack quickly, but I know she's thinking of that worst thing too.

"I've got one more client in—damn!—two minutes, and then I'm clear. I was going to do administrative work today, but it can wait. Today's all yours, OK? Just sit tight. I'll be down soon. There's still tea in the pot."

She grabs the old teapot and sets it, slopping, on the table. I stare at it so she can't see my eyes. She can do this mind-reading telepathy, given eye contact.

She's hurrying now, which helps. "It's only 'cause I love you. 'Cause of what you've been through. You know that, right? We'll talk at lunch, OK?" She kisses the top of my head hard, as if I'm eight years old, and hurries up the stairs.

I wait till I hear her professional spiel kick in on the phone. "Sarah Mayfield speaking. Good morning."

I nip into my room and get changed, fingers clumsy and hurrying.

Tick, tick, tick . . .

In less than a minute I'm ready, in a compromise outfit of short-sleeved purple tunic dress over leggings. It'll pass for normal, but I can still move fast in it.

I creep downstairs and sit on the bottom step to pull my running shoes on. Lacing them up, I feel stronger. Putting on my running gear always does that. It's like a superhero outfit, that spandex, and I need it more than ever today.

I remember the first time I told Eden I'd joined the running club, last February, when I started back at school. Running hurt. Everything still hurt, back then, but at least it gave me something to focus on. Something I could make progress with.

"Hill running? Since when? That's so not your look!" She'd yelped with laughter, till she saw my face.

"Oi, you know I'm good at running—it's not a fashion statement."

"But once a week—really? Bor-*ing*! All that effort, just to sit around afterward, boasting about times and *personal bests*." She stressed this last in a nerdy voice. "Not my idea of fun."

"E, if I'm fast, I can get away." I spelled it out for her. "I need to be the fastest. It's all I've got. After what happened, I need options: fight or run. And I'm not doing martial arts." That shut her up.

She even came to watch me race a few times, cheering me on at the finish line.

Now that I'm all ready to run, I grab an empty backpack

and tiptoe back into the kitchen. I feel like a thief as I shove my hoodie, some energy bars, and a water bottle in there.

I grab a pen and peel a sheet of notepaper off Mum's pad of sticky notes. I scrawl: *Sorry. I had to. I've got my phone.*

I hate sneaking out, but I've got no choice. Holding my breath, I open the door slowly and slip through, closing it carefully, noiselessly, behind me. Someone's on my side, 'cause it doesn't squeak or slam. Mum's office is at the back of the house, so she won't see me. I take a deep breath, pulling as much air as I can into my lungs. Then I begin.

I run down the street and take the track up through the woods to Eden's. I try to picture what I will find at her house. I fail. What Eden's parents are going through is beyond imagining.

.　•.•.•　••

It was a Saturday morning, June 4th. A slice of blue sky split the curtains. Mum brought me a cup of tea and put it carefully on my bedside table.

"What's up?" She usually lets me sleep. "Mum, what's wrong?"

She was sitting sideways, awkward, on the edge of my bed. She stared at her hands, not looking at me. I read the angle of her neck, the tension in her shoulders. This was horribly familiar. I sat up. "Mum!" My heart started to race, chasing away my sleepiness. "What's happened?"

She took a deep breath as if she was getting ready to dive. "Oh, Jess, I'm so sorry. I've got bad news." She reached out and grabbed one of my hands and said it in a long rush: "There's been an accident. It's Eden's sister, Iona. She was killed last night in a car crash."

The words reached me very slowly.

Their meaning hit me afterward.

Like thunder a few seconds after lightning.

"What? No!" My hand sealed my mouth, and I spat it off again, feeling nausea rising with my confusion. "Where's Eden? God. No, was she—"

"Eden's all right, Jess. I mean, she's not, she won't be. But she wasn't in the car."

Eden wasn't in the car.

"Oh God, her poor mother . . ." Mum hugged me so tightly that I could hardly breathe, and I finally understood what she had told me. We cried on and off all that day, damp-faced, red-eyed, and shaky. We cried for Iona. We cried for Eden and her parents. And we cried for us, and for our own near miss last year. I needed not to be far from Mum, and she must've felt the same about me, so we shuffled around the house, making food we couldn't eat, and then we sat on the sofa, watching old films that made us cry again, with the curtains still closed, letting the perfect day go to waste.

I kept getting my phone out to start a text to Eden. I deleted each attempt savagely. What could I say? What was the point of words today? But some words had to be better than no words, so I eventually sent:

So sorry, E. I can be there in 10, just let me know? Love you. Jx

Then chucked the stupid phone down and sobbed for being so inadequate.

But Eden didn't reply. Death closed around Eden's family like a big black fence with Keep Out notices.

I missed Eden at school. I kept walking past conversations that were shushed into silence as I got near, and suddenly I had courage to face the gossips, 'cause it wasn't for me, it was for Eden.

"Yes, it's true."

"No, she wasn't drinking and driving."

"Have a bit of respect."

In the middle of the second week, Mr. Barwell read out a letter to our homeroom group, from Eden's parents, Claire and Simon, that began "We are devastated at the loss of our beautiful daughter Iona. We invite her friends to celebrate her life with us . . ." and ended with the time and date of the funeral.

. : ⦁ : ⦁ ⦁

So there we were, a ragged knot of kids, parents, teachers, milling around by the iron gates of the chapel on the hill. Not sure if we should be there. Wishing we didn't have to be there, not for this. So tense and nervous we hardly dared speak. Katie Sutcliffe was at the front, Iona's best friend, her face already swollen and blotchy with tears. Everyone sweltering in black on the hottest day of the year. My heart was a panicky helium balloon, bumping and rising inside me. My senses were muddled, working overtime. The blue June sky stretched tight from hill to hill, pressing down on us like a lid. Everything was too bright, too sharp: HD unreality.

I felt the change as the black cars pulled up: everyone bracing for this.

A white coffin was hoisted into view. It wobbled forward on the shoulders of Simon, Eden's dad, and five other men I didn't know, all wearing the same expression of desperate concentration. Eden and Claire came next. I hardly recognized them. Death had done this to them, made them as distant as celebrities, flat as cutout paper dolls. They clutched each other, tissues like crumpled white flags in their free hands, and I couldn't tell who was holding up who.

This had to be wrong. Surely this was where I woke up? *Eden, Eden, I had the strangest dream.*

We blundered into the chapel in their wake.

"I've got you," Mum said, gripping my elbow as she steered me into a row at the back. I couldn't look at the coffin, or I'd have to realize what it held. The service passed in a blur of heat and tears. I focused on the worn wood of the pew in front of me, counting all its little knots and scars. My chest ached, iron lungs. Katie managed to read a poem. They played Iona's favorite song. That's what undid me. Mum and I filled tissue after tissue, trying not to make any noise.

Afterward, the coffin left first, then the mourners followed row by row, in a strict hierarchy of grief.

We beetled after them, a black stain spreading over the churchyard, toward the place they'd prepared. I wobbled, grabbing at Mum, my head full of snot and cobwebs. The brightness hurt my eyes. I wanted sunglasses, but it felt disrespectful. I saw buttercups like broken glass, glinting on the grass. Bees groaned past in the hot still air, the noise grating on my nerves.

"OK, love?" Mum whispered, and I nodded, lying, feeling the pressure build.

We huddled around the deep grave, where they'd spread fake grass to hide the mud. They started to lower the coffin on fabric straps. Eden, Claire, and Simon stared, eyes wide, mouths open, faces rigid with horror.

I had to concentrate on something, or I was going to lose it, and it wasn't my place to do that. I named the colors of the earth's rainbow layers as the white box descended: emerald, loam, rust, cream, ocher, jet.

Someone was reading prayers.

Claire flung a handful of earth. It clattered on the bone-white lid. On the plaque reflecting light and sky. It looked wrong to dirty it up. Iona wouldn't like that: Her room was always so neat.

Eden froze, soil in her hand, staring down. Long moments passed. People started to murmur.

The look on her face was an electric shock, zapping me back to life. This was what I was for. This was real. I crossed to her and took one side. Liam appeared at the other. I hadn't even seen him till now. He looked older in his black tie.

We each passed a hand around Eden's waist, tinier than ever in this black dress. I felt her sag against us. Her fingers sprang open, scattering dry little clods of soil over our feet. She gazed down at our shoes in a row: my boots, polished up for today; Eden's low slingbacks; Liam's shiny new lace-ups.

"It's OK . . . Come with us, it's all right," Liam whispered. "Hold on."

Moving as one, we maneuvered Eden backward. The sea of black parted for us. We stumbled down the slope and found a place near the long grass at the edge of the graveyard. We sank down, looking out over the summer valley, at the farms and the distant hills beyond.

Nobody spoke. We held her. I could feel Liam's arm below mine, the warm fabric of his white shirt.

I would get her through this. I would save Eden's life, like she saved mine. Nothing else mattered. Not school, not exams, not parents, not work. This would be Eden's summer. I would do anything to get her through.

I looked out at the patchwork of green fields, at Stoodley Pike pointing to heaven in the far distance, at the kestrel hovering above us like a witness, and I swore my vow.

PART TWO

CHAPTER FOURTEEN

12:05 p.m.

Sorry, Mum. Sorry, Mum. I hate running out on her like this. My feet beat out the apology, sending loose stones skittering, till I'm halfway up the hill and I can let it go. Trees curve over the road, creating cool, green shade that smells of earth and fallen leaves. Even today, running helps. It makes my fear the second thing, because first there is this:

Each breath, pulled hot from my chest . . .

My stride, feet pounding earth . . .

I lose myself in the effort of it, breath, muscle, eye, foot, falling forward and pushing on, on, on. I leave the trees behind and hit the last steep bit. It's hotter here and I have to work at it with piston arms.

When I'm nearly there, I stop to catch my breath so I won't burst in all sweaty and gasping. I take a minute to lean on the nearest wall, finding a patch of warm stone not smothered in brambles all heavy with ripening blackberries. I push back, stretching my calf muscles while my breathing slows.

As soon as I stop moving, the thoughts crowd in. Will Claire and Simon let me in? Will they be angry? Do they think it's my fault?

I sigh and trudge forward, dreading what I'll see at Eden's house. I feel like I'm wearing some kind of iron corset made of fear, tightening around my ribs with every step. I look around me, hoping I'll see something Eden dropped, anything to give me a clue, but the lane and the fields are empty. Up here the sky feels bigger, out of the hemmed-in valley. The hills sprawl away to the moors at the distant horizon, where tiny pale wind turbines spin in a row, like beach toys. The fields and woods are deep green, clinging to summer, and the warmth rises off them, bringing a scent of baked earth and heather.

I reach the top of the hill. There's a row of wind-bent trees and a line of stone buildings along the ridge: four farmhouses, hundreds of years old. Eden's is the third one along. The stone is worn, all the hard edges smoothed away by lifetimes of wind and rain. As I get near, the dogs in the neighbor's yard go crazy, barking and throwing themselves at the gate.

Claire opens her door at the noise and comes out. I see the strained hope in her face as she scans the lane in each direction. "Eden? Eden?" Her voice sounds thin and high.

"No, sorry. It's only me," I call. Seeing her face collapse with disappointment nearly makes me turn round.

"Oh, Jess, I thought . . . Has she . . . ? Have you . . . ?"

"No." I shake my head, hating to see the last trace of hope erased. "I'm sorry, Claire. I needed to come . . . I wanted to say . . ." What exactly? What can I possibly have to say to her when she's living her worst nightmare? Only the need to find Eden stops me from running back down the hill.

Claire's looking at me with a desperate hunger in her pale-blue eyes, as if I'm the one who's going to conjure her daughter back, right here. She looks thin and older than before, in her loose green sweater and jeans. I can tell with half a glance that she hasn't heard any news, good or bad. She's still waiting, every nerve strung tight. "What do you know, Jess? What did she tell you?" One bony white hand shoots out, and her fingers are cold where they grip my arm.

"Nothing. I mean, nothing new. She seemed all right yesterday." I blush, the feeling that I'm a complete letdown overriding my reaction to her touch. Claire's fingers release. I make myself ask the question that's been buzzing around my mind like a wasp trapped against a windowpane. "Mr. Barwell said you had a text from her. What did she say?"

Claire's face slams shut now. "You shouldn't be here, Jess. But now that you are, you'd better come in." Her tone is sharper. She turns and disappears into the dark shadow of the doorway.

I follow.

Inside, the house looks the same—same bright living room with its huge arched window, same massive squashy sofas where me and Eden have watched so many DVDs, curled together like two kittens. It even smells the same—flowers in a vase on the piano, fresh coffee drifting in from the kitchen. But the wrongness of it all overwhelms me. Eden's new absence and Iona's older absence are the biggest things in the room, pushing out all the air. I wrap my arms around my rib cage, ignoring the iron corset, and try to breathe normally.

Simon walks in, holding a piece of paper. "Jess?" He's tall, and I always thought you could see he was Eden's dad, in spite of his darker coloring. For a moment I think he's taking it better, that he's not as crushed as Claire. Then I meet his eyes and see how wrong I am.

"I want to help," I blurt. I feel stupid. "I mean, I've just spoken to the police. I know they're doing everything . . ."

"They're sending a family liaison officer. Should be back any moment," Simon tells Claire.

She doesn't react. She crosses to the mantelpiece and picks up her phone to check the display. I wonder how many times she's done that today.

"Jess, where would she go?" Simon halts, folding forward and grabbing the back of a chair. "We've been over and o—" He gasps as if he's been punched.

"I wish I knew. I want to look, though. I mean, that's what I'll do today. I'm going to look for her."

He nods and straightens up. His skin is gray against the white of his crumpled shirt. "What do you know about Liam Caffrey? He says he brought her home last night." His voice is tight and bitter, forcing out the last few words as if they tasted bad. "Seems upset. Puts on a good act."

"It's not Liam," I tell them both, as gently as I can. "Please, you can't think that. Whatever's happened, it's nothing to do with him."

"Well, who the hell is it to do with, then? Because someone out there knows where our daughter is." Claire's voice is unrecognizable.

"Did she tell you about Tyler? From the party last Saturday? Has she mentioned him?"

"What? No, she hasn't. Tyler who?" says Simon. "He was in my house? You mean, he knows where she lives?"

"Do you think it could be him? Why aren't you telling the police? You can't just walk in here and throw names at us, Jess. Don't you realize how important this is?"

I flinch beneath Claire's rage. It was a mistake to come here. They don't want to see me. Their grief is too big: It's a tsunami, overwhelming. I'm no help to them, unless I find Eden. I need to stop talking and just do something.

"I did tell the police. Please believe me, I'm trying to help. Tell me if there's anything I can do."

"The police said they'll need a photo." Simon sounds like he's barely keeping control. "Something about a media strategy."

"What about the one from her online profile? She likes that one." I chew my lip.

"We don't even know what she was wearing, but that Caffrey boy gave us a list. You might as well check it, Jess. Does that look about right?" Simon puts one hand to his eyes, as if he can press back tears, and holds out a bit of paper with the other.

I scan it—cropped jeans, red T-shirt, black hoodie. "Yeah, think so." But there's something wrong. My brain is trying to tell me something, but I can't hear it in here, with all the deafening absence.

The silence grows between us. Three little islands of pain in this big room. I've no idea how to speak to them today. Not so long ago, Claire and Simon were like anyone's folks, making polite conversation when I came for tea. Simon making crap dad-jokes. Claire bringing us snacks. June changed that forever, but this is beyond worse. What happens to them now? Who will they be without Iona and Eden?

I can't bear the way they're looking at me. "Should I take a look in her room? I might notice if anything's missing. I mean, if she packed a bag or something."

"Will you? I've tried, the police have searched, but you might see something different. Just don't touch anything. The police said . . ." Claire's already turned away to pick up her phone again.

I go up the stairs and along the corridor, past Iona's room, and then I pause outside Eden's. There's a glass frame of childhood pictures hanging on the wall between the two doors. It's like they're mocking us. Eden and Iona, potbellied blond toddlers in matching yellow sunsuits on a foreign beach. In their old garden, the house before this one. The riverbank nearby, where they always went. I touch the glass covering the photo. There's Iona aged ten, giving Eden a piggyback ride, laughing and squinting against the sun, all skinny brown legs and knobbly grazed knees. Eden and Iona, frozen in time. Happy together.

The photos dislodge a memory.

The last time we all went to the riverbank together. We must've been twelve, Iona nearly fourteen, at the end of the summer holidays. Iona and her best friend, Katie; Eden and me. A whole day at the river. Iona was in charge. I remember she was bossy—rationing out the sandwiches, giving us challenges—but she was kind too. She carried the heaviest bag. And she found soothing dock leaves for my nettle sting. I remember me and Eden pretending to catch fish. Iona and Katie climbed ahead, downstream to the shadowy pool hidden by the rocky overhang. Rays of sunlight shafted down, bouncing off the water, reflections of reflections, casting rippling veins of gold everywhere. We found Iona and Katie curled up together on the same shelf of rock, so their hair was tangled, light and dark entwined, whispering secrets, their feet dangling in the water. Mermaids.

When we got close, Eden whooped and scooped a glittering wave of water, soaking them both.

"Oi, I'll kill you!" Iona shrieked, but laughing, not cross.

"Well, you did just say this was heaven!" Katie told her. Then we all started play-fighting, splashing and sliding right into the water in our shorts.

I remember Iona pulling Eden out when she got too deep. I remember her arms, wet and slippery, around her sister's neck. I remember them hugging.

. . : . .

I go into Eden's room. Inside, it's bright and still. The curtains are open. The bed hasn't been slept in. The whole room looks unnaturally clear—you can't usually see this much carpet. Claire must've tidied as she searched. But it's still shocking, like Eden's been neatened away already.

I look around me, trying to work out if anything else is different.

The walls are covered with posters—three of her favorite bands, two vintage film posters—and over her bed, the vast bulletin board covered in photos, postcards, notes.

"Like Pinterest," she'd said, "only, y'know, with real pins . . ." There were photos ripped out of travel magazines: Machu Picchu, New Zealand, Cambodia—places we were going to go together one day. There's the card I gave her on her last birthday because the girl on the front looked like her. It's hanging open and I can see the sign-off and the cake I drew: *Big love with cherries on top, Jess xxxx*.

My heart clenches again, and I push down the panic. I need to stay focused. What would she take if she was running away? Her tablet sits dark and blank on her desk, on top of a pile of school textbooks. Her iPod is in the speaker dock. I sit on her bed and feel under the pillow: The T-shirt she sleeps in is there.

Eden hasn't run away. She would have told me. Whatever might be happening with her folks, she couldn't leave me, not now.

"E, where'd you go?" I whisper to the empty room. "Is it 'cause of Iona? You know it's not your fault. Thought we'd done that one. Come on. Come back. We need you."

And maybe it's just my lonely synapses firing crazily, but for a moment I'm sure she can hear me. Eden's right there.

Folded arms, that stormy blue-gray light in her eyes, the jut of her hip, frowning at me, warning me.

I blink. I have an idea. I know I'm not supposed to touch anything, so I wrap the fabric of my tunic awkwardly over my hand and tug open her bedside drawer, where I know she keeps her diary. It's not there. As I'm looking down, I see a flash of silver catch the light, something small at the edge of her bed. I reach down, and my fingers close on something hard and cool.

I lift it for a closer look: In my palm is the small twisted lock from Eden's diary. Someone broke it open. I dive onto my hands and knees and check under the bed, but there is no sign of the diary.

Who broke the lock? And when?

At the same moment I hear the sound of a car coming up the lane, and a footstep in the hall squeaking on a loose floorboard. I manage to get up just as Claire comes in the room, hoping my face isn't flushed. I wrap my fingers around the broken lock.

"You know what?" she says. "I even heard her come in. I'm sure I did. I never go to sleep till she's back. Unless I'm going mad . . . I was waiting up, in bed but awake and listening, till she was home. I heard the door, heard her move a chair in the kitchen, so I let myself fall asleep."

She moves and sits on the bed, smoothing Eden's pillow. "Till this morning. She didn't come down, and then I found her room like this. . . ." A small gasping sob escapes. "No one knows what that's like. Not unless they've been there . . ."

I'm mute. I have no words for this. Tears fill my eyes, making Claire a pale shimmering blur.

"It's our fault," she says. "We shouldn't have left her last weekend. We should've insisted she came too. But she said she was fine. She's stayed on her own once before. . . ."

My heart lurches at the mention of last weekend. If we're doing guilt and last weekend, I'm going to win. "No," I tell her softly. "It's not your fault. . . ." I rub my eyes to get rid of the tears.

"We've been so wrapped up in our loss, we haven't been there for her." Claire's speaking almost absently, staring at the bed. She looks up and seems to focus with difficulty on me. "Did she ever say that to you?"

"Nothing like that, no. I promise." I look into Claire's eyes, even though it hurts to see the raw pain there, willing her to believe me. And the last thing I want is to make it worse, but I've got to know. I need to understand. "But can you tell me: What happened with Eden and Iona? I know Eden found something out, but she didn't tell me what it was. When she found her birth certificate, something about Iona . . . ?"

Claire springs up as if the bed is burning hot. I see her lips turn white as she draws them tight. "Get out," she says quietly.

It's worse than if she'd hit me. Biting back fresh tears, I hurry down the hall and back downstairs. "I'm sorry. I don't want to stick my nose in. I'm just trying to help," I babble, but it's no good.

Claire herds me out, her face all pale skin, empty eyes, and her mouth pulled in a tight line. "Jess was just leaving," she tells Simon, but he doesn't even raise his head.

Through my tears I focus on my feet, stumbling toward the front door. The sight of Eden's sandals, lined up next to her new boots, nearly finishes me.

Claire opens the door and there's a police car pulled up outside. Two officers are climbing out, a man and a woman—not the two I saw this morning. Their neon jackets seem very bright. A radio crackles at the woman's belt, but she ignores it. Then another man gets out from the backseat. He's wearing a suit.

I hear Claire's sharp cry next to me, before she collapses slowly, sinking against the doorframe.

They tell us they haven't found Eden. They send me away. Claire and the police watch me leave, faces closed tight: locked, barred, and shuttered with suspicion. I blunder down the hill, taking the other, rougher route, stumbling over potholes and tripping on rocks as big as my fist. The tears won't stop. I fall downhill through a tunnel of trees, on the dark side of the valley, where the sun doesn't reach.

This hillside is bleaker, half-covered with straggly trees and burnt-orange bracken. There's a ripple of movement in the deepest dappled shade and I dart toward it. *"Eden? Eden?"* It comes out a broken screech.

The answer explodes in my face, bronze wings battering. I guard my face with my hands, crouching low to dodge the mad clattering panic of a pheasant. It flaps past, squawking its alarm call loudly, and roosts in a small hawthorn to escape me.

The adrenaline surge gives me wings too. I turn and take the corner too fast. I slip on loose scree, heel jutting in a long forward slide. I land on my back in a mess of gravel and dead leaves, skinning the back of my arm.

For a long moment I just lie here, listening to the blood pound in my ears, staring up through shivering beech leaves at the distant blue sky. I'm still clutching the tiny metal lock from Eden's diary.

And I realize that if we don't find her, I will never, ever forgive myself for what happened last Saturday night.

 # CHAPTER FIFTEEN

Liam led me, hyperventilating, away from the surge of bodies on the dance floor. My mind clutched at three things, keeping it small:

1. *Keep breathing*
2. *Don't faint*
3. *Follow Liam*

I focused on the back of his head, noticing how his hair was cropped in a very straight line above the deep golden tan of his neck. We jostled through the open doorway and I gulped down the cooler air gratefully.

In. Out. In. Out. One foot in front of the other. He was holding my hand, and my world shrank to that as I tried to make it a positive. His hand was bigger than mine. His palm was warm. His fingertips were slightly rough, shaking with tremors to match my own. He cradled his other hand against his chest. The knuckles were bleeding and a darker stain spread across his faded red T-shirt, as if he'd been shot.

I didn't know which of us was in a worse state.

We passed a blur of people, lights, laughter in the darkness. We walked deeper into the gloom, along a crooked paved path. Liam took a left, down steps to the secret garden. Eden must've shown him this. It was a circle of lawn with a plum tree right in the middle, heavy with fruit. All around grew dense rhododendron bushes, so it was completely hidden from every angle, but we could see out over the moonlit valley below.

"Here." He let go of my hand. "Take it easy, Jess. We're safe here, right?"

Was he asking or telling? I collapsed back, crushing the long grass, cool and damp under my fingers. I stared up at the stars. The sky was blue, not black, and there was a moon rising over the opposite hill, three-quarters full and very bright. The moonlight made wisps of cloud glow like pale party streamers in the sky. Stalks of grass and round silvered dandelion heads hung over my face.

In. Out. In. Out.

"Breathe," Liam said, as if he could read my mind. Apparently satisfied I wasn't going to stop, he lay down next to me, a safe distance away. He folded his arms under his head, then swore as he scraped his injured hand. "Can you name them?"

"What?" I said when I could speak again.

"The stars. Do you know them?"

I knew he was trying to distract me from the panic attack. "Only the ones all kids know. Big Dipper. Orion."

"Always liked Orion. Ready for action. Dude with the sword."

"Dunno the rest." I tried to play along, even though it felt surreal, even though my speech was hoarse and halting. "I know they're supposed to look like animals and gods and stuff, but it's just a big swirl. 'Cept that one there. That looks like my cat. Constellation of Fluff."

Liam laughed, a short bitter cough, but still a laugh. The sound of it was like a safety rope for me to follow back to earth. "What about that one?"

"Yeah, it's a bus."

We kept at it. He told me the real names and I'd tell him they looked like a kettle or a sausage or something really ordinary.

We ran out of ideas eventually. An owl hooted somewhere near us. I was feeling nearly normal now. Distractions worked for me. I hoped the distraction Eden had chosen was giving her a break too: It had to be worth something.

"Is your hand OK?"

"It's nothing."

The silence stretched out between us.

"She doesn't mean to hurt you," I said finally. I heard him fidgeting, ripping up grass and twisting it in his fingers.

"Maybe."

"Definitely. It's not even about you, is it? Just distraction. Stuff to blot out the bad."

"Yeah, well. Tonight was different. With that lad—Tyler. Who the hell is he anyway? And in front of everyone, showing me up. Maybe it's time to call it quits."

"No. She needs you." I roll on my side, leaning my head on my arm, trying to make out his expression in the darkness.

"Nah," he said. "She needs you, not me."

"Well, it's easier for me. I'm her best friend, now and always. But don't you go leaving her 'cause of tonight."

"I dunno, Jess. I've put up wi' it for months. Maybe I've had enough. Maybe I want something else. Maybe she does too— tonight is proof of that."

My heart leaped with hope, but I kicked it savagely down again, denying it.

He ran his bloody hand over his face. "God, what kind of jerk does that make me if I walk now? Don't you see? It has to be her. It has to be Eden who calls it, not me."

What could I say that had the ring of truth? "People know you didn't sign up for this."

"Neither did she!" he hit back on the next beat. "It's just what happened. It's not her fault, and I should stick it out." He balled up the shredded grass and chucked it away as if it was a hand grenade. "What about you?"

We didn't do this. We talked about Eden and how she was. We didn't talk about us.

"You OK? I mean, really? Back there, that was 'cause of . . . ? Y'know, what happened to you?"

I was glad it was dark and he couldn't see the rush of blood to my face. "Yeah. Not good with crowds and stuff." I knew everyone knew: It'd been in the papers with the court case.

"Bastards. I'm sorry, Jess. It shouldn't have happened to you."

My eyes had adjusted to the darkness. I could see his face in the dim light. He'd changed again: back to angry. Back to bloody lethal.

"I swear, if I ever get near one of them, I will *kill* them for what they did to you."

I believed him, but this whole Jekyll-Hyde act didn't make me feel any better. I didn't need anyone's righteous vengeance. It wasn't flattering. It was all violence: same as what they'd done to me.

"Wrong place. Wrong time. Wrong hair. Wrong clothes." I grated out the words I'd learned to say.

"Nah, don't. C'mon, it's me. *Cut to the truth*, remember?" His hand reached out and stopped in midair, dark against the star-filled luminous sky. "You can be honest with me. We're a team, right?"

"Right." It was true. We'd been a united front this summer. A good team at work. A good team as Eden's caretakers. He was Eden's boyfriend, so I felt safe with him. I let my guard down. I let go of my shield, shrugged off the armor. I didn't have to hide with Liam. It didn't matter if he saw me, because he was spoken for, his eyes fixed firmly on Eden.

"OK." I exhaled long and slow, finally letting go of the tension I'd held all evening. The panic attack was gone, leaving me beached and heavy. The earth below me felt strong and safer than any person I knew. It held me and I let myself relax in that embrace. "OK, then, Liam Caffrey, you want to cut to the truth?" I told it to the stars. The truth tasted hot and powerful as the whiskey in my glass tonight: too strong to take neat. I organized my pain into a careful, edited list.

"One: Bad things happen for no reason. It's shit and unfair.

"Two: It's my business. I don't need you or anyone else talking vigilante nonsense about killing people and revenge.

"Three: That doesn't mean I have to forgive them. Don't see why I should."

"Fair enough," he said, back to Mr. Reasonable. I couldn't keep up with the mood swings.

"Really? You don't think I'm bitter and twisted and in need of professional help?"

"Nah, Jess. I think you're brave. The rest, it's normal, in't it? You get hurt: you bruise, you bleed. It's what happens. This is the same."

I sat up so I could check his expression again. "Thanks. Most people want to keep their distance, in case it rubs off on them, my bad luck." I wrapped my arms around my knees, hugging them in.

"Yeah, well. Not me." He sat up too. "But it'll get better, like a bruise does." He held out his right hand in a fist, squinting at the damage, admitting it. "Like this will."

The clouds shifted from the moon, giving us more light. His eyes held mine. They seemed very big and shining. I couldn't read them.

"Do you wanna talk about it?" he asked me.

His hand reached out again, but didn't stop this time. My breath caught in my throat as he touched me.

Liam tugged at one of my hands to release it. Then his

finger brushed the inside of my left wrist, light as a dandelion head on the tattooed skin. For some reason, this didn't trigger my usual response. Instead, his touch anchored me. It made me feel safe.

"OK," I told him, surprising myself. "You want the whole story?"

He nodded.

CHAPTER SIXTEEN

Last November really outdid itself. After the minor sparkly compensation of Bonfire Night, it was a month of hard work: triple homework each night, accelerating toward the end of term. It got dark earlier every day, and the light was rubbish for painting. I didn't want to be late with my art coursework, so I was working through my lunch breaks. Eden came around to my place after school most nights and we did our homework together.

This particular night, it was wet, cold, and windy. Mum made veggie shepherd's pie and apple crumble. Me and Eden took second helpings 'cause the weather seemed to demand it, then couldn't finish them: completely overwhelmed. It was after nine when Mum put her head around my bedroom door. "Isn't your mum going to be wondering where you are, Eden?"

"Yeah, s'pose." Eden stayed where she was, leaning on the radiator, stroking Fluff curled in a tight white circle next to her.

I knew Eden preferred being at our house these days. It kept her out of Iona's way. Their war was getting worse all the time.

Then she smiled at Mum and started getting her stuff together. "Thanks, though, for dinner and everything."

"Anytime, Eden. You know you're always welcome here. When's the next bus? Don't want you waiting in the rain. I'm sorry I can't drive you—our car's in the garage again."

"It's all right." She checked her phone and turned to me. "There's one in ten minutes." She gave me her best pleading face. "Walk me to the bus stop, J?"

"Really? In this?" I could hear the rain splattering out of our gutter onto the street below. "And you can save the puppy-dog eyes, E. They don't work on me." It wasn't true. She knew I'd give in. She'd ask, I'd agree. That was our dynamic. She led, I followed, and it worked fine for both of us. What did I want to be out in front for anyway?

"Ah, go on. What if it's late? Anyway, I've not finished telling you what Josh said today."

"All right, then, seeing as it's you." I got up too and followed her down the stairs. "But I want it noted: I don't get soaked to the skin for just anyone, Eden Holby." We put our coats on, hardly dry from the walk home. Then I turned and shouted through the open door, "Mum! Be back in ten, OK?"

We ran, yelping, through the rain, seeing as neither of us owned an umbrella. They were testing the flood sirens. That eerie distant wail always freaked me out; it sounded as if it belonged to wartime.

"Hurry up, E, you'll miss it!" The raindrops were heavy on my shoulders and my hood, little scrabbling paws trying to get in.

We went along the main road and then ducked under the underpass, where the back lane was pouring with water off the hill. From there, it was a sharp left, up the ramp onto the station forecourt, with Eden's bus right there, waiting to head off in the opposite direction.

I yelled, "You owe me one, E! Tomorrow!"

She ran for it, with a backward wave. I saw the bus pull away, Eden safe inside its little warm bubble. She put her face up to the glass and made a stupid face, eyes and mouth wide as a clown's.

I laughed out loud—with the rain pouring down my cheeks, I bet I looked like a clown now too—waterproof eyeliner and mascara were no match for this—and then I turned for home.

I hurried back down the ramp. I pulled my hood lower, now that I was facing the wind. I didn't see the people coming under the railway bridge till they were right in front of me.

Six or eight of them, shouting and smoking, heading slowly for the station.

I hunched my shoulders, avoiding eye contact, and did a quick check behind me to see if I was OK to step into the road. I gave them a clear foot, dodging the two girls nearest me.

But just as I passed, one of them stepped back, screeching with laughter. Arms flailing, she slammed straight into my shoulder.

"Oi, you blind bitch!" She yanked my hood down but didn't let go of it, or the clump of my hair that she'd grabbed in her fist.

Rain in my face, heart pounding, I tried to pull away. The second she let go, I'd be out of there and they would not catch me.

That didn't happen.

My scalp burned. I felt hair ripping away. "Get off me!" I screamed. Both my hands flew up, trying to push her away.

My hand connected with warm soft flesh. Her face? Her neck? All I knew was that her fingers released. I spun, gasping, ready to run.

"She fucking winded me. Get her."

The others closed in. The rain wasn't bothering them. They had all the time in the world for this.

I had time to think, *This is real, this is actually happening*, before her boyfriend moved in, filling my vision. Tall, blundering, doughy: He had a shaved head and boy breasts filling the shiny Manchester United shirt under his sodden jacket. His eyes narrowed with drink and hate at the sight of my face, my Sky Blue hair, my piercings.

I smelled his pickle breath as he came in for a closer look. I held my hands up, reasoning with him. "OK, I'm sorry. I didn't mean to hurt her, but she was . . ."

He flicked his cigarette away. I remember noticing how neatly he did that, between middle finger and thumb. Then he pulled his arm back and punched me in the face.

My head exploded. The pain was massive. It pushed every other thought away: blinding, crushing, awful. I collapsed. Wet hands and knees. The cold reached me distantly. My vision smeared with orange and black. I twisted my head and vomited, bringing more pain. Above me, the rain broke over the street-light like an asteroid shower.

"Fucking dirty goth."

That twisted drawl, rattling out words like bullets.

"You're not fit to touch her. Emo scum."

My reactions were too slow. I pushed back onto my knees and tried to stand. I thought they'd finished. I'd touched his girl. He'd hit me. We were done here.

I went to get up, but there was something wrong. My body didn't move right. If I could just get up . . .

The lad jerked back, but not like he was leaving. His weight shifted backward, with focus and momentum, like an Olympic high jumper . . .

His foot connected with my ear. Something cracked. The pain was worse.

Nuclear.

A mushroom cloud of pain blossoming, red on black.

Moments passed like years of pain.

I was flat again. Standing seemed ambitious, but I tried to crawl away; I knew enough to try to crawl away. "Please . . . Don't . . ." My fingers slipped on warm stickiness and cold concrete.

A girl's foot appeared right next to my face, in a black, heeled boot. I could see the scuff marks on the toe. Was this help? Was this finally someone coming to stop it? I squinted up, searching for a hand, something to grab, a lifeline.

"Here," she said.

My heart heaved with relief.

Then it hit me: a warm gob of spit, right across my face.

The boot disappeared and kicked my hands away. My chin hit gravel. The next kick left me gasping: fish on a slab. I curled up. Hands over head. Whatever I did, I left something exposed and that's where they hit me next.

Chest. Back. Shin.

Rib. Rib. Cheek.

Pain went off the scale. There had never been pain, till now.

I heard a shriek like a vixen. Laughter.

"Car!"

"Come on. *Now.*"

"End it."

Hands lifted me and I groped blindly, like someone capsized. Which way was up? A crack of vision returned. They swung me out into the road, toward the tunnel. A car coming.

A car.

Rain in headlights.

Light.

Light meant help.

By the time the driver saw me—arms out, blinded by blood, flying forward, creased double—it was too late.

I slammed into the hood.

Fade to black.

CHAPTER SEVENTEEN

Light returned in flashes.

Sirens.

Mum's face, white as paper.

Pain was the sea I floated in. Sometimes the waves were high; sometimes it was calmer.

Machines bleeped. Voices came and went.

Tides of confusion finally receded, leaving me beached and gasping on a strange gurney.

I felt Mum's hand touching my forearm. Stroking it. Cotton sheet under me. Pressure around my head. One hand felt strange. My body felt stranger.

"Where are we?"

"Emergency room."

"Why?" The pain said it was me that was hurt, but I needed to check. "Mum, are you OK?"

"*Jess!*" she sobbed. "Don't you remember?"

I sank beneath the waves of pain again.

Next time I woke, everything was cushioned. I bobbed on the surface of the pain now instead of sinking.

"Is that better?" Mum asked. "They've given you stronger meds."

She stroked my elbow.

It was morning now. There were curtains around my bed. I could hear people moving. Someone was groaning.

I flicked my eyes the other way. There was a window with a smooth silver catch. White sky full of clouds. The rain had stopped. *Rain.* I almost remembered something, but it twisted away and I was too tired to chase it.

"Oh my Jess," Mum said. I'd never seen her like this. She was limp, flat, 2-D. "I love you so much," she said, kissing my elbow.

What was it with my elbow?

My head felt weird. My fingers were in padded gloves. I wrinkled my nose. Mistake. I breathed in and shifted my weight, trying to sit up. Big mistake. The pain shot off the scale.

I started to panic. What was wrong with me? What was wrong with my face? My hands? I got it now. She was kissing my elbow 'cause it was the only bit of me that didn't hurt.

"Mum? What happened?"

"You've had a CT scan, love. You've got two broken ribs. Your fingers are sprained, not fractured, they said. They've stitched up your face. And your ear. They had to shave off some hair, but it'll grow back in no time. . . ."

"No, I mean, what happened before? Did we crash?"

The look of horror that crossed her face nearly finished me off.

"You really don't remember?"

So Mum gave it back to me, all the parts she knew, from the driver of the car and what my injuries had told the doctors. I had to watch her suffer it, all over again. When she was finished, that made me hate them even more.

.   •   ?   • •

We went home.

Strange days came next. I slipped in and out of sleep. For someone who'd been in bed for days, I was surprisingly tired.

Dad, Rachel, and the twins came, all the way from London, while I was still very groggy from the meds. Dad tried not to cry in front of me, but through my bedroom wall afterward I heard Rachel comforting him as he sobbed. The twins were scared of me, and who could blame them, with my bandages and my Darth Vader wheeze? They stood next to my bed and stared at me, perfectly matching, with their beautiful round brown eyes and golden Afro pigtails. Hope gave me her lucky heart-shaped white pebble. Esther tried to give me Mr. Dog, her small saggy comfort toy, stained beyond recognition from nearly six years of hard loving.

"No, he'd miss you too much. He's a city dog," I managed to whisper. When I opened my eyes again, they were gone.

Weeks passed. Christmas happened to other people. Mum sat with me, chatting, reading, silent. Sometimes, Steph was there: I heard her talking with Mum downstairs. I ate her cooking.

Mum took down the bathroom mirror. She wouldn't let me see the damage, not yet. I didn't need to. I could see myself reflected in her face. I knew we were both wrecked.

. •. • •• •

I was a cracked egg. My brain was a sieve. First I couldn't stay awake: exhausted 24/7. Then I progressed to exhausted *and* restless. Jumpy as a box of frogs. Rattling with painkillers. Now I didn't want to sleep because of what waited there. I told Mum not to let anyone come round, but she chose her moment to ignore me.

"Jess? Can I come in?" It was Eden's voice.

My tidal wave of panic rose—nothing new, it came crashing through twice a day at least—making my throat dry, my stomach twist. If I hadn't been slumped on the sofa, my jelly legs would've joined the panic party.

I heard Mum whisper, "Go on in," and then, "Jess? It's Eden!" as if I didn't bloody know. Mum fussed in, zapping the TV to silent, tugging the curtains open.

"Mum! Back off. What are you doing?" I flinched from the light like a vampire, furious with her. It was too soon! How dare she decide when I was ready to see people?

I guessed what she was playing at. The doctor had hinted I should be doing better by now. The physical therapist said I could take on *more of my daily activities*. I thought the psychologist looked plain worried.

I turned my head into the cushions so I wouldn't have to see Eden's disgust when she looked at me. If I'd known, I'd have put on makeup, a scarf, anything to hide behind.

"Hey, J," Eden's voice said quietly, somewhere near my unmangled ear.

I waited for her to ask me how I was, so I could laugh.

"Thanks for letting me visit. I've missed you. People send love. Here . . ."

Rustling.

Not a card. Not a pity card signed by the whole class. *Please.*

"Magazines. And I went to the candy store on the way up, got all your favorites in a grab bag. And . . . some DVDs, new ones we've not seen."

I didn't move.

"I'm not staying. Mum and Iona have gone on some lame museum trip, and I'm going to the football game with Dad."

I hadn't even known it was the weekend.

"But anyway . . . I'll come back on Monday after school, if that's OK?"

I didn't speak.

Her hand found my hand. Her little finger managed to wiggle its way around my little finger. Our secret signal from years back, from primary school. She squeezed once and waited.

I couldn't do much, but I could do that. I squeezed back.

Monday after school, Eden was back.

I was prepared this time. Full makeup, right up to the edge of the cotton scarf I'd wrapped around my head. The fabric covered most of the mess. So what if it made me look like a cancer patient?

And credit to Eden, she didn't even blink at my freak-chic. She acted as if nothing had changed. "Hey, J. So they made me bring you stuff: updates on the lessons you've missed, and homework." She pulled a folder out of her bag and tossed it on the floor. "What you do with that is your business. I'm not saying a word. I'm just the messenger pigeon." She turned and smiled, looking directly in my face.

It was too much, like sudden sunlight in a dark room. She was too much. Too normal. Too much energy. She hurt my eyes and I had to look away.

"Hey, guess what. New lad in Year Twelve. Geeky but gorgeous. Imo's taking aim . . ." Eden launched into a stream of school gossip. When it ran out, she looked around my bedroom. I knew it was a stinking pit. Piles of books and zines. Crumpled tops and leggings strewn on the floor. Cups of tea turning gray under the bed. Old toast furred with mold. It was a battleground between me and Mum, but this week I was winning. This week I was very angry, and I couldn't blame her for backing off.

"So your mum reckons you're doing really well. She said maybe we could go for a walk?"

Double take. I hadn't left the house in weeks, unless Mum was driving me to a doctor's appointment. I hadn't left the house *since*. And I wasn't doing well. I wasn't doing anything.

"No."

"Why not?"

I stared at her.

"You can walk, right?"

"Yeah. But it still hurts."

"Jess, you can't stay inside forever. We won't go far. I'll be with you. Just to the end of the road?"

Why was she doing this? She had no clue. Had Mum put her up to it? I needed to hide. I couldn't go outside. Couldn't she see I was broken? Stuff happened outside. Those people could hurt me, outside.

Actually, those particular people couldn't hurt anyone else, anywhere, since they'd been caught on the station's security camera as they legged it for the train. Plus, witnesses heard them boasting about bashing an emo, saw the bloodstains, called the police. They were arrested off the train as it pulled into Manchester Victoria station.

It didn't help.

Then I had a thought: If the pain got worse, I could take one of the strong pills, the ones that made me sleep so deeply I didn't dream.

"OK."

She looked pleased. "What do you need me to do?"

I let her help me up. She was good at this, I realized with surprise. Patient. Letting me go at my own pace. Asking me what I needed instead of guessing.

It took a while to get downstairs.

"We're going out." I said it harshly, still cross with Mum.

"OK, love. Got your phone?" she said, in a voice that might've sounded normal to anyone else. She looked so grateful she might cry, but I knew full well she'd be pacing like a caged lion till I was back safe.

As I started down the hallway toward the front door, pale winter sunlight pouring through its glass pane, I began to doubt if I'd make it. I used the wall for support and my sweaty palm left a damp smear along it. My legs were shaking so hard I had to stop.

"You can do it, Jess," Eden said, behind me. "Listen, it's never going to be this hard again, right? The first time only happens once, so let's get it over and done with."

"Who put you in charge?" I muttered, but I latched on to her words. She was right. I didn't have to go far. Then I'd be owed one of the good pills and I could hide for the rest of the day.

I put my hand on the door handle and pulled it open.

Air, light, and sound broke upon me like waves crashing down. A car going past. Birds singing. Footsteps and voices coming up the road. So ordinary, so overwhelming.

I stood there, sucking in cold lungfuls of air.

The last time I did this, we went out into the dark and rain. We ran, laughing, down the road. We had no idea what was waiting for me.

What might be waiting today?

"I can't," I said, half turning.

"Yes, you can." Eden blocked the doorway. "Come on. Just a few more steps. Just to the end of the street?"

I shook my head, gasping, wondering if I could dodge past her like a rugby player. Was this madness? Was I crossing the line into complete, barking insanity?

"Jess, please?" Eden crumpled, losing the attitude. "I want you back. I know you can't help it and you can't rush it, but *please*? Just take the first step so I know you're coming back, and then I'll wait, as long as it takes, I promise . . . Jess, *please*. I can't bear it, not when it's my fault that it happened."

That shocked me into stillness. "What?" I couldn't even work out what she meant by that. But the begging landed better than sternness. Eden needed me. Maybe I could do this for her, even if I couldn't do it for me.

My cat dashed through my legs, as if he knew I needed someone to follow.

"OK." I inhaled. The cold air on my cheeks was raw and unforgiving. I stepped down off our doorstep, into our little terraced street that ran uphill, at a right angle to the main road at the top. I stood, shaking, on the weathered flagstone outside the house. I felt naked, exposed, an insect wiggling madly with its wings pulled off.

Nothing happened.

Fluff stood there, nose twitching in the cold air, and then he stalked off up the street with his tail waving.

Eden offered her arm and I grabbed it. Like two old ladies, we trudged slowly up my street. I looked at my feet, in boots instead of slippers for a change. I kept my head down and plodded, counting the steps to hold it together. My ribs were on fire. Sweat trickled down my back. My head hurt badly—going off like a fire alarm wired into my brain. Finally, we reached the top of the street.

I stood there panting, trying to accept that this was my life now. The old Jess was gone. This trembling ghost girl was what I'd become. I looked around me, clinging to Eden as if she was my life raft. A few kids were playing, farther along. A white van was parallel-parking opposite. Monday teatime, nothing special.

If we turned left, in a minute or two we'd be back there, where it happened.

There, in the rain, seeing them approach . . . their laughter . . . I had to run. I had to flee.

"No!" With a moan, I pulled away from Eden's arm. Panic gave me wings. I stumbled, and then I ran. Adrenaline surged through me. I made it back to the house in seconds, falling through the door, into the hall, into the kitchen.

"Jess? Jess? What happened?"

I sank down in the far corner, against the fridge. I pulled my knees up and curled tight, ignoring the pain as I creased forward.

Eden tumbled in. "I'm sorry! I'm so sorry, Jess. You weren't ready. I shouldn't've pushed it."

I buried my head on my knees and made a noise I didn't recognize. A ball of pain and fear. Eden and Mum knelt down, one on each side. There with me. Living through it, with me.

Eden was right, though. It was never as hard again. And that mad dash back to the house? That's what first gave me the idea that I needed to be fast. I needed to be able to run.

CHAPTER EIGHTEEN

"There you go. The full story, Liam Caffrey." I wiped my face. "The Unfortunate History of Jessica Mayfield." Salt tears in my scar, again.

He'd held my wrist the whole time. Even when his eyes filled too. Even when a tear ran down his cheek and dripped off his chin.

Now he let go, just for a minute. He grabbed the loose front of his old red T-shirt and used it to wipe his face. "Blood, sweat, and tears, today, eh?" he joked softly. "Oh, Jess."

I looked at him fiercely. I did not want his pity.

"It's the past," he said. "It's done."

"It's not. The scars won't go. Not completely. Not ever."

"So? Nothing wrong wi' scars." Liam held my wrist again and bent to it, closer, lower. His cropped hair was white gold in the moonlight. He paused. "We've all got 'em."

I lifted my wrist to meet his mouth. He kissed me, soft and warm, on the exposed skin. On my racing pulse. Afterward, again, he waited. He held my wrist and watched me.

There was no one to see, just the bright swelling moon and the laden plum tree and the hidden owl in the wood. We could hear the distant bass and voices spilling from Eden's party.

It was me who moved. My hand touched his cheek, saying yes. His face. His cat's eyes.

I screwed my eyes tight shut. The look in his eyes was too much. I reached for him blindly. My fingers crossed his chest, its warm drum beating faster. I stroked his bare arms: the warm skin, the solidness of him. My fingers danced up his neck. My knuckles grazed his cheekbones. One fingertip crossed his lips, and he kissed it.

His breath, warm on my ear, sending shivers down my spine. That breath, catching, jagging, speeding—just for me.

His fingers moved up my arm, tracking the lines of my tattoos, taking time over each one. I had a million nerve endings I'd never known about, more than stars in the sky. My skin was alive and breathing again. My skin wanted to be touched.

He sought out my scars. I felt his fingers, coarse at the tips but so gentle, lightly sliding across my face to where the skin was ridged. He caressed the wave of scar tissue by my ear.

I opened my eyes then, to check this was real. My eyes on his. His eyes on mine. And the air between us, so close and thick. Like the tension before a storm, it crackled. I felt it, between us.

There was still time. I could break the spell. I could move away, not much harm done. Just the line between us crossed and we knew it. He waited for me.

I held his gaze as I crossed it again. I lifted his hand and kissed his knuckles, shredded and torn.

I kissed him because I wanted to. I kissed him because I needed it. And when he kissed me back, that was it. I didn't know anything else, except his mouth on mine and our hands moving, and time flickering and flowing around us so smooth and so fast, like the river running deep over rocks.

CHAPTER NINETEEN

1:25 p.m.

A call from Mum jolts me out of it. I don't know how long I've been lying there under the beech trees, playing back Saturday night. . . . I hit REJECT, then dust myself off and limp down the hill into town, ignoring the voice mail alert that follows. I look down at the jumble of terraced houses, the zigzag roof of a warehouse, the shops, churches, movie theater, park. All basking in the afternoon sunshine, all looking unbelievably normal.

I see Liam's sister Nicci across the canal as I take the shortcut down a flight of stone steps. She's sitting on the fire escape of the club where she works, smoking a cigarette. The sun stripes the side of the tall brick building and she's got her eyes closed against it. Her hair is piled up in a high hairdo—strawberry blond, same as Liam's.

"Nicci!" I shout and wave, and she raises her cigarette in a lazy salute.

Liam was lucky with his family. He was the baby, with a gang of older siblings all looking out for him. He told me and

Eden once, "Most of them have gone off the rails somewhere along the way, so there's nothing I can do that will shock Mum now." I liked that Sharon wasn't shockable. I remember her piercing two-finger wolf whistle from the back of the school hall when we finished primary school. How the uptight parents flinched.

Then I see Liam.

He's coming down the middle of the street, also heading for Nic. I brake and watch, ignoring my heart.

He's changed into jeans and a blue T-shirt, but it still doesn't look like him. Liam usually walks all loose and easy, but today he's hunched up, as if he's carrying something heavy on his broad shoulders. I want to shout to him, but my mouth is sandpaper.

I speed up, rushing over the bridge and around the corner into the short, dead-end street, with our old primary school filling nearly one whole side. Gothic and Victorian, its windows are plastered with artwork, filtering the high-pitched twittering of kids on a Friday afternoon. People dart across the quiet street like swallows, diving into the post office, clutching packages to mail.

Liam sees me and slows. "Hey." Something crosses his face, but it's written in a foreign language and I can't translate.

"Hi. You been home?"

"Yeah, police came round."

"Same here. Whole interrogation scene?"

"Yep." He sighs and closes his eyes against the light, leaving his eyebrows to tell me the truth. He looks terrible. His face is pale, in spite of the tan, and his eyes are circled with shadows that look more like bruises. The freckles across his nose and cheekbones stand out against the pallor. Light catches on the soft golden stubble on his cheeks and top lip.

Seeing him hurts more than I expected. Of all the people in all the world, we must be feeling the same today, but it doesn't help.

I want to hug him, but there's a force field pushing us apart. He's awkward, hands in pockets, shifting his weight from one leg to the other.

Eden's there, laughing at us. "You should see yourselves," she taunts. "Honestly, the pair of you! If there's a job to do, just do it! Don't tangle yourself up in knots."

He opens his eyes, ridiculously blue, under those thick brows, darker than his hair. It's like he can't bear to see me without Eden. He covers his face with both hands and rubs his face and head, making his short hair stand up in little tufts.

I have no idea what to say next. Words turn to soggy crumbs in my mouth.

Nicci walks down the fire escape to join us, her heels clanging on the metal stairs, and we both focus on her with relief.

She glances at her phone, lights another cigarette, and says briskly, "I've only got ten minutes, so we need to be quick. Fill me in. You went to school as usual, right?" she prompts.

"Course. It was a normal day, till . . ."

I wonder who told him: Claire or one of Josh's Neanderthal mates? Maybe the first he heard of it was from Trent?

"Then, after Barwell and Trent's little session first thing, they sent me off home to talk to the police."

"Mr. Barwell?" Nic checks. "I remember him. He used to be all right. He'd have your back, hear your version?"

Liam shrugs. "Barwell's OK, but Trent made her mind up about me years ago. She made it sound like I was the prime suspect or something. Anyway, back at our house, the police took my story. Good thing you saw me come in last night, Nic, or I'd be cooked."

"You'll be fine. You're innocent. And we will find her. How did it end?"

Nicci seems focused and practical. It calms me, but works the opposite effect on Liam. His lips wobble and pull downward. His eyes fill with tears.

"Hey, come here. It'll be all right." Nicci does what I can't do. She pulls Liam into a hug right there in the shadow of the fire escape. I watch her hands with their long aubergine nails, deft and capable: One holds her cigarette out of the way while the other pats Liam's shoulders.

She lets him go and passes him a cigarette. "Here." She lights it for him and they both lean back on the brick wall.

"How was it, then?" I move closer, wafting away their smoke. "What did they ask?"

"It was awful." He squints at me, shielding his face with his free hand. "They thought I'd done something to Eden." He takes a hard drag on the cigarette. "Fucking feds, jumped to the worst conclusion. 'Cause of, y'know, Clarkson."

"What about Clarkson?" I'm missing some facts here. "What happened with him?"

Nicci swears. "I'm so sorry, Liam."

"It wasn't your fault! It's Clarkson's. No one does that, not to my sister."

Nic smiles at him and ruffles his hair.

I join the dots, wondering if I'm seeing this picture right. "Did he hurt you, Nic? You mean Josh, Eden's ex?"

"Nah, he didn't hurt me, but he tried."

"Nic turned him down, so he waited for her outside the club to show her what she was missing. Didn't realize I was two steps behind."

"Oh. *That's* why you hit him."

He looks at me and it's complicated.

My mind works fast, trying not to jump to conclusions, but here's a new possibility: What if Josh Clarkson got to Eden somehow, took out his jealousy? And all that swagger this morning was cover-up?

"Mum gave the police a right telling-off again today," Liam is saying, with a shadow of a smile that vanishes instantly. "As if me laying out Josh Clarkson's got anything to do with this. As if I'd hurt anyone. As if!" He exhales hard, sending out a long stream of smoke.

"I know that." I can't imagine what he's feeling. This is bad enough without anyone suspecting I might have hurt Eden. I mean, physically. "So will you tell me about last night? What did happen?"

"I swear, Jess, I dropped her at the top of the lane. She

didn't want me coming to the door. The farm dogs make a right racket. Didn't want to wake 'em all up. But I stayed and I watched her walk away and she waved when she got to the door. I told them. I told them everything—that we'd been in the park, then here in the club after. Stayed here till half past eleven. Didn't believe me till they got the alibi from you, Nic."

I tell them what Claire said, about hearing Eden come home.

"OK, so tell me the timings again," Nic says. "You got in at half past twelve, so you must've left her, what, midnight-ish?"

"Midnight, just after . . . something like that. I left her. I came home. Had a smoke with you, crashed. End of. That's it, Nic, that's all I know, I swear!"

"I know, I know," she soothes.

"But what was she like? How was she?" I blurt. What had changed between me leaving her at the park gates and midnight?

"Y'know." Liam shrugs, avoiding my eyes. "She didn't want to talk much. Bit hyper, maybe. Not as bad as Saturday . . ."

He and I both flinch.

"I mean, she wanted to do stuff, keep moving. After the park, we had a few drinks, we played pool, we . . ." He pauses, then blurts, "OK, so we might've had a fight."

A fight? My heart stutters and jumps like a stuck CD.

"It's all right," Nic tells him, giving me a look that makes me wonder how much she knows. "Did you tell the police?"

"Yeah, some. People heard us yelling. I said, yes, we'd fought. No, she wasn't bloody suicidal. And there were no sketchy blokes stalking us in the shadows. How was I supposed to know she would disappear? I'm not effing psychic."

Me and Nic are silent, waiting for the ripples of that one to disappear. I think about the tarot reading again. *Hope ahead*, it promised. I could really do with that coming true about now. I can't help seeing the other image: the grim reaper.

"So what do we do?" he demands. "What the hell do we do now?"

"We've got to get it on social media. I've seen it work," Nic says. "You post her picture and the facts, ask people to share it. Come on, come up wi' me now. You can use the club Wi-Fi and get it done quicker." She stubs out her cigarette and kicks it into the gutter.

We follow her through the weathered red double doors and up the winding stair. The back bar is empty except for a bearded bloke reading a newspaper and he doesn't look up when we come in. There's sunlight streaming through the high windows, and soft folky music on the sound system. I've never seen it so quiet.

"The boss is in the office through there, so make it quick, OK?" Nic goes behind the bar and starts putting away the clean glasses.

Liam and I take the nearest table. We pull out our phones and face each other. You could cut the tension with a giant chain saw.

Tick, tick, tick . . .

I know we should hurry, but I've got to say something. We've got to get past it. Surely it's like pulling off a bandage:

Do it quick and it'll hurt less. I want to ask what they fought about. Instead, I say, "Did you tell Eden about Saturday?"

"No!" His denial is so loud that Nic looks over in surprise and the clinking of the glasses halts. Beardy Man frowns over his paper at us.

"No! Did you?" he hisses at me, leaning in. I see the rising flush in his cheeks and I know I've got one to match.

"Course not." I burn up under his gaze. For a long moment we stare at each other. Then I make myself say the right thing: "Look, let's forget it happened, right? Let's just put it behind us."

It's not what I want to say. It's not what I dreamed of saying. My mind's already designed a dozen fantasy scenarios for me and Liam, but since not one of them involved Eden going missing, they're all just hot air and wishful thinking, and I stab at them so they pop and shrivel like little balloons.

"We've got to focus on finding Eden. Deal?" *She didn't know! They didn't fight about that. So it's not 'cause of us that's she's gone!*

"Deal," he mumbles, glancing over at Nic to see if she's listening.

The awkward tension shoots off the scale.

"OK," I say, ordering myself to get a grip, "let's do this. So I'll save her profile pic—" I flick through apps on my phone and talk through what I'm doing—"and share it, saying: 'Missing, Eden Holby. Last seen just after midnight Thursday, early hours of Friday'?" I check and he nods. "'Please phone West Yorkshire Police—'"

"Wait. I've got a number. Police gave me this." Liam fishes out a crumpled business card, same as the one I've got, and reads it off to me.

"OK, tagging you . . ." His phone beeps as it comes through. "Done. You do one."

While we're busy, Nic brings over Cokes and packets of chips, and I realize I'm starving. Breakfast seems like it happened a lifetime ago, to a different person.

We work at it for a bit, clicking and forwarding. When I'm done, I look down at my phone, at Eden's face smiling up at me. She didn't know when that photo was taken that one day it'd be used for this. I shiver, feeling cold suddenly.

"Jess,"—Liam calls me back to reality—"you're right, we *can* do this. If we work together, we can find her, OK?"

I swallow down the worst thoughts. "OK. Right." But the panic won't leave me. I've wasted time today. I haven't found out one useful thing. And all this time, Eden could be lying somewhere, hurt. She could be lost, she could be . . .

"See what I found?" I tell Liam, digging the little metal lock out from my pocket. "I think it's from her diary. Someone must've broken it open."

"Guess you can't blame her mum for doing that today. But it might've happened any time. Iona could've done it months ago. It doesn't have to mean anything."

"What if there's stuff in her diary that we need to know? It might help us know where to start, who to talk to."

"Jess! Enough. She's out there somewhere, so let's just get out there. Let's start looking. At least we'll be doing something."

He is looking at me with a strange expression on his face. "Let's start at the waterfall. Last time we went, she said it was her favorite place."

"OK." It was on my list too.

"And there's tonight. It's that full-moon party, up the valley. We can walk back that way. I was supposed to be DJ'ing. Forget that. But we need to be there, to ask around."

"Yeah, that makes sense," I say, trying not to dwell on how Mum is going to react when she finds out. We'd always wanted to go to a full-moon party, me and Eden, only we were never allowed: too late, too remote.

At the full moon or solstice, some hard-core party people would drag a sound system up to a clearing in the beech woods. They'd rig up decks and speakers in the ruins of an old mill, and hundreds would come to dance: all sorts, Liam'd told us, balding ravers next to teenage kids and everyone in between.

"She really wanted to come tonight," Liam's saying. "She was gonna sneak out. We'd planned it."

"Where is she?" I burst out, unable to hold it in any longer. "Liam, what the hell is going on?"

"You know what I think?" he says slowly. "I think someone knows. She must've gone out again. Either she met Tyler or she ran into someone else."

I sit there, wondering what that means and why Eden hadn't told me. Then I wonder just how much she'd had to drink and what state she was in, without me there to look out for her.

One night in July, Eden had persuaded me and Liam to stay out late with her. We'd had to leave the club in a hurry after Eden almost started a fight. Me and Liam did the apologizing and got her out of there. We staggered over the little canal bridge, the two of us like two tugboats pulling Eden along.

"You can't go around telling people stuff like that," Liam said to her.

"Yeah, but it's true. She *was* out of his league. And she was so giving that other lad the eye." Eden was slurring her words and it took both of us to keep her on track.

"Yeah, but if you piss him off, and I come over to back you up, then it's him and me facing off. . . ." Liam sighed and ran his free hand over his face and hair, tufting it up. He did that at times of stress, I'd noticed. It was warm, and he was in shorts and tee. "Don't you get it? If it all kicks off, it's not just you who gets hurt. There's me. And there's Jess, Eden. Remember us?"

Eden pouted at being told off. We'd reached the other side now, moving slowly along the canal path, by the park railings. "Oh, yeah, sorry, J. We're still doing eggshells and tiptoeing around our precious Jess."

"You what?" I turned to her, stung, letting her arm fall. Let Eden keep herself upright, then, if she was going to insult me.

"Just saying, it's been, what, six months since, and it's like it was yesterday. Surely that's wallowing?"

"Eden . . ." Liam saw my face and tried to stop her.

"I'm not going to wallow." Eden wasn't even looking at me. She stood there, swaying gently, in her short green cotton dress. The front of the skirt was damp where she'd spilled her drink. Her face was pale, her eyes unfocused. "I'm not going to let this stop me. My sister does not get to derail my summer—"

"Eden, you're drunk. Let's go." Liam spoke loudly over her. "Move it on."

I swallowed down my hurt. I took a long moment—deep breaths like the psychologist woman taught me. When I was calm enough to speak again, I kept it practical. "All back to my place. Eden, you can't go home like that. Liam, I need you to help me."

"I can walk! Get off me, you fussy pair. Mother hens! Ha!" Eden was taken with that image. She started squawking and flapping her way along the path, but at least she was moving again. For a while. She petered out after a few steps and flopped over the metal bars that edged the canal.

Me and Liam came in and took one arm each, like some bizarre four-legged race. Liam had most of the weight. Our bare arms met across Eden's back: warm skin. I tried not to pull away too sharply as I readjusted, shaking my bracelets free. We slowly moved round to face the stone steps that led to the road. Eden put her hand up and stroked my hair as we set off again.

"Ah, Jess, your hair is so soft. Feel that, Liam? You'd think all that dye wouldn't help, but it's so soft. . . ."

"Yeah, whatever, thanks, E."

"So soft . . . But why do you keep dyeing it? You don't make it easy for yourself, do you, J?"

"What do you mean?" I asked, bracing for the answer she'd give me in this state.

She stumbled and clung tighter to my neck. "Well, why do you dress like that—like the bride of Dracula—if you don't want to get picked on? I'm not judging! But it's the obvious question."

I halted and she slammed sideways into me. Behind her, the canal was still and black, reflecting orange streetlights.

"What the hell . . . ?" I couldn't swallow this one down like I usually did. This time I was white-hot furious. "This is me, E. We can't all look like our town's next top model, and quite frankly, you're not looking too great yourself right now."

"Hey, easy! Easy." Liam tried to come between us, looking freaked out. "She didn't mean it, did you, Eden?"

"She'd better bloody not have. Because it sounded like she was saying it was my fault, what happened. *My fault*, for looking the teensiest bit alternative?" I gestured at my clothes: black jeans, long black tank with the red print, not so extreme. "Not their fault for being aggressive Neanderthal morons who'd slam anyone who wasn't like them!"

"I'm sorry, J. I didn't mean it," Eden said. Her drunkenness was a pale mask, only I wasn't sure who was beneath it anymore. Her mouth was slack, her hair getting tangled in her face. She was a mess. She was more of a mess than me.

I couldn't stay angry. It'd be like kicking a toddler who'd tripped over. I waited, searching for a line to make it OK. "Good, 'cause you were beginning to sound like you'd swapped bodies with some old git. Trent maybe."

"Urgh, Jess. You're twisted." Liam jumped gratefully onto the change of topic. "So you're saying I've been kissing Mrs. Trent? The Tank trapped in Eden's body?"

Eden went even whiter. A hand flew to her mouth, "Oh, no, I'm gonna throw . . ." She whirled round and leaned over the rail, puking into the overflow channel between the canal and the river.

"I've got this. You wait up the steps," I told Liam. She wouldn't want him seeing her like this.

Liam backed away, mouthing, *You sure?*

I nodded, holding Eden's hair out of the way and rubbing her back gently until she'd finished. Then I rummaged in my backpack for a water bottle.

"Eurgh. I hate that," she groaned eventually.

"Here, hold your hands out." I poured water on them so she could wipe her face.

She spat one last time, then turned and folded into herself, sliding down onto the ground and resting her pale face on her knees. "You're good to me, J." Without opening her eyes, she reached out one damp hand. "Best friends?"

"Yeah, E. Best friends," I replied, squeezing her cold hand gently.

We got Eden safely back to my place and up to my bedroom without waking Mum. We put her in what we thought was the recovery position, a sick bowl near her head, and covered her with a sleeping bag. We sat, one on either side of her, watching over her like slightly tipsy guardian angels. Though there was nothing like seeing your best friend vomit an entire evening's hard drinking to make you sober up fast.

"Did she drink this much, before?" Liam asked.

"No. Some, at parties, but not like this," I whispered. The room was dim—just the glow from the blue glass lamp on my desk. I looked across at Liam, his long legs tucked up and his arms wrapped around his knees. It was very quiet: just the three of us, breathing. His eyes were large and dark, staring at me.

"Maybe it takes the edge off it all."

"Yeah, and who's gonna argue with that? As long as we're with her, she'll be OK."

"You'd better take my number," Liam said, uncurling and pulling out his phone. "Use it, anytime, OK? If she needs us, we cut to the truth, right? No mucking about."

In whispers we made a pact to work together, to tell it straight, so we could be there for Eden.

Only, somewhere along the way, we must have failed.

CHAPTER
TWENTY

2:30 p.m.

Liam and I walk to the bus stop in silence. The force field pushing us apart gets stronger. I'm feeling paranoid and exposed, like I've lost a layer of skin. We have to wait for the bus and every second is agony. I am sure the whole town is watching us and judging. People pass, doing ordinary Friday afternoon things: going to shops, bank, library, taxi stand. I watch and judge them right back. How can they carry on, when Eden is missing?

My phone rings. It's Mum, again. I ignore it.

Tick, tick, tick...

Liam slouches next to me against the grimy graffitied plastic, looking at his phone and fidgeting till I want to scream at him. Blink once: He's Eden's anxious boyfriend, desperate to find her. Blink twice: He's a twitchy young man with a history of violence. Someone with something to hide.

What was I thinking, last Saturday, to take my eyes off Eden? To do anything that might hurt her? Why hadn't I seen how fragile she was? The tarot reading on Monday should've been my wake-up call. But she fooled me at school, all bright and breezy, and I was happy to let her, if it meant she didn't know about me and Liam. I'd acted along with her, all bloody week.

This isn't an ordinary mistake. This might be the biggest fail of my life. I slump there, miserably accusing myself, spinning out into a dark and hopeless pit. When the bus finally comes, I barely look up. Liam gets on. I hear him paying for us both, so I have to follow.

The bus is empty, apart from an old couple and a woman with two little kids and a stroller. Liam slides onto the back row and I sit down next to him, regretting it instantly. I cannot be this close to him. My leg touches the edge of his jeans and I jerk away, but I'm too uptight to move seats. The bus heads out of town. It's one of those local roads that was never meant for the twenty-first century and the bus driver has to play chicken, dodging in and out of parked cars, braking hard and zooming suddenly if there's a gap, scraping through the narrow places with barely room to spare.

I'm thrown against Liam with every swerve. I peek sideways. He's looking straight ahead, his arms rigid, gripping the seat in front. Being so close to me is clearly an ordeal for him too.

Finally the bus leaves town and heads for the moors, where the road is wider. In my mind I run through everything I've learned so far, revising the gathered facts. Eden went home, got changed, and went out with Liam last night. They were at the skate park and the club. People must have seen them there.

Around midnight, he took her home. Claire thought she heard her come in. And then something happened. By this morning she was gone. So far, so nothing. What else do I know?

I make one of my lists, only it's not positive, it's negative. It's the worst list in the world—all those who could've hurt Eden:

1. *Josh Clarkson*
2. *Tyler*
3. *Some random stranger*
4. *Liam Caffrey*
5. *Eden Holby*

I need to start by ruling people out and then see what's left.

Liam has a temper. The evidence is right in front of me— his knuckles are healing, but they're still dotted with scabs and clouded with old bruises. When he cracks, he does it spectacularly. He's admitted they had a fight last night. Could Liam have hurt Eden and then deny it so well? I look at him and right now it's not very hard to believe. I know he can lie. And with that scowl, he looks furious again. I can see the tension in his forearms, the outline of his bicep through his T-shirt. If he wanted to, those arms could hurt someone.

Could Liam have hit Eden if she pushed his buttons badly enough? He once hit Josh Clarkson for threatening Nicci.

What did that say about Clarkson? Was he looking for a way to get back at Liam? How far would Josh go to punish Eden for leaving him?

What about the new lad, Tyler? He was Eden's choice last Saturday. Did he come looking for her? I know almost nothing about him and it's driving me mad.

I remember something.

"Liam! Liam!" I tap his arm, awkwardness forgotten. "What was Eden wearing on her feet?"

He looks at me as if I've gone mad. "I dunno. I did the list for Eden's dad—jeans, red top, black hoodie . . ."

"Yeah, I know, but what about her *shoes*?"

"What about her shoes?"

"It's important. I saw something at Eden's today." I don't want to give him options in case he just grabs one to shut me up.

"It's not the kind of thing I notice, girls' shoes."

I tut. "Oh, come on, drop that crap. Just think!"

"All right, if I have to, it was probably her sandal things."

"Color?"

"Maybe red?"

"That's it. That's what she was wearing at school too. But they're at her house. So either she was barefoot or she changed into something else. What's she got?" I ran through the list: She had other sandals, slingbacks, flip-flops, sneakers . . . Why did she change her shoes in the middle of the night? Or was she barefoot when something happened? That hurts to think about.

Liam's ignoring me. He's gone somewhere inside himself, staring out of the window.

I notice with a jolt where we are, press the bell, and jump to my feet. "It's our stop."

We get off and start down the little side lane that leads to the waterfall. I'm so lost in thought I just drift after him.

When I come to, Liam has pulled way ahead of me. He's striding fast, and his shoulders are stooped under all that weight. Soon he's just a little stick man on a narrow road to nowhere. I let him go.

Either side of us, the moorland is broad and sloping. You can see forever up here. You can see where glaciers carved out the valleys and smoothed the hills. The fields flow down like breaking waves. We're so high it's all sky, plunging fields, and lonely moor, just that ruined barn on the opposite hill. It's the kind of landscape you either love or hate. It's majestic or it's oppressive. It could drive you mad—all the miles and miles of emptiness reminding you how small we are.

The track loops around the shoulder of the next hill and Liam vanishes. I remember what happened last time we were here.

.•.:•.•

Early August, the weather picked up again. I was working the lunch shift at the café, feeling my shirt sticking to my back.

Liam came in to collect his wages. "Hey up, Jess. Bit quiet, isn't it?"

"Duh. Anyone with any sense is outside." I spoke quietly, but the only customers—a couple at the back table—weren't listening to us anyway.

"That's where I'm headed. Sorry. Only an hour to go, eh?"

"Yeah, but it's not exactly flying by. Dev's got me multi-tasking." I pointed at the line of plastic cups on the countertop. "I'm supposed to be naming the new range of smoothies. Then drawing it all up on this blackboard." I gestured at him feebly with an orange chalk.

"Good luck with that. Hey, did you see Eden last night—how was she doing?"

"OK, bit quiet, but all right, I think." This is what me and Liam did now: spoke most days, swapping notes. It was two months since Iona's death and nothing Eden did was predictable. "She had a new box set; we watched some o' that. You seeing her later?"

"Dunno. She's not replied yet." He pulled his phone out to double-check. "You want a hand with this, then?"

"God, yeah. I'm stuck. Everything sounds lame. Mango Madness? I mean, really? Problem is, they look like poisons. . . . My head's stuck on a crime theme."

He came around the counter to join me, eyeing up the drinks.

"More like Killer Kiwi?" Liam said, getting it.

"Here, what about this one?" I handed him one. "Try. It might be your last mistake," I said in my best film-trailer voice.

He took a sip.

"Strawberry Silencer?" I timed it so he'd just swallowed.

He spluttered, spraying the countertop with bright pink gloop.

"You've done it now. Dev'll go mad. That so contravenes all his favorite hygiene regs." I grabbed the antibac spray from the sink and pointed it at him. "Freeze!"

Liam was still coughing, so I slapped him on the back, giggling. "I did warn you!"

"What's going on here?" Eden's voice carried across from the open doorway. "Having fun?"

We straightened up, lost the laughs.

Eden came slowly closer, looking from my face to Liam's and back again. "I thought you weren't working today, Liam?"

"I'm not, just collecting my . . ."

"He's not, just helping me with . . ."

We spoke at the same time and then petered out. I felt like a guilty kid caught stealing the best cookies.

An awkward silence followed.

"So, anyway, now we're all here," she said breezily, "*together* . . ."—I could hear her forcing it—"look at the weather. So, what are we going to do?" Eden demanded.

"Er, still working over here?" I said, wiping down the countertop.

"Come on, let's get out there. We've got to make the most of this summer. You know, before it hits us."

"What, exactly? The unbearable pointlessness of exams year?" I smiled at her to dispel the awkwardness, glad to see her smile back. I leaned on the counter by the till. "So what's your plan?"

"We'll go to the waterfall. I brought towels, spare bikini, come on!" She knew how to tempt me.

"I'm in," Liam said, walking around to join her. "But you can keep your bikini, ta very much: I've got shorts. And there's leftovers, Dev said. We can have a picnic."

Dev was super strict about use-by dates and we often got day-old stuff to take home. "Looks like a proper feast."

"Yay! See, it was meant to be. And guess what I've got," Eden whispered, eyes shining, gesturing at her backpack.

"Magic monkeys to fly us there?"

"Champagne! I nicked two bottles."

"Yeah, 'cause your folks have got an actual wine cellar. Flippin' heck." Liam rolled his eyes but squeezed her in a quick hug.

"Come on, then," Eden said.

"Jess's got an hour to go. Why don't we help her finish this?" Liam suggested.

Eden didn't seem to hear him. "Let's go to the park while we wait." She was already heading for the door.

The next hour went very slowly. I finished naming the smoothies with cheerful kids-party lettering and tried not to wonder what Eden and Liam were doing.

After my shift, we caught the bus up the hill. The late-afternoon air was so thick and golden it felt like warm honey on my bare, patterned skin. We rushed down the narrow stone path, squeezed between two green fields, pushing back the Queen Anne's lace that hung down into our faces.

My excitement grew with the noise of the falls. I'd been coming here all my life: It symbolized the best of the summer holidays. When we arrived, there were just a few families left, packing up. Soon we had the place to ourselves: the basin of water and the sheeting white falls. There was a circle of perfect blue sky between the high banks, edged with green leaves where the sycamore and silver birch trees leaned in, moss and ferns on the lower levels.

It felt like a magic spell fell on us then. Maybe it was the light: that syrupy golden warmth, with seeds and blossom floating around through the haze.

Eden had a rug. "This is it. We know how to do it in style. Towel for you, Jess!" She chucked it over with her spare bikini. I managed to shimmy into it under my dress.

Eden was stunning in her white bikini, showing off her golden tan, and I tried not to mind how milky my skin looked next to hers. Liam stripped to his shorts. I averted my eyes.

"Liam, go stick this bottle in the river, for later? It's gotta be cold as ice."

When he was back, Eden looked at us with a serious expression on her face. "I want to, y'know, propose a toast. I know it's not been easy for you two, putting up with me this summer—"

"Hey, don't say that," I butted in.

"Don't interrupt me! It's hard enough as it is." Her eyes were big and bright and I could see this mattered to her. "I just wanted to say thanks. And you're the best. Cheers!" She lifted the bottle and then popped the cork before we could reply, spraying us both lightly with fizz.

"Cheers!" I leaned in and kissed her cheek, tasting suntan lotion and salt, our sunglasses clashing. "And you're welcome," I whispered. "What else would we do?" Then she was passing me the heavy bottle, sun glinting off its gold foil.

Afterward, we all leaned back on our elbows in the sunshine. The light made rose fractals on my eyelids. The champagne made my body hum with warmth. The best bit of the magic spell was Eden and her good mood. She was her old self, like before Iona died. Funny, but not unkind. She never used to be unkind.

"What could be more perfect? Being here with my two favorite people," Eden said, lying back and closing her eyes, her fingers finding Liam's on the rug.

Liam was restless. The champagne turned his dial up three notches. He couldn't sit still and he couldn't stop talking, endlessly changing the subject. "Hey, did you hear Dev banging on about his new menu yesterday?" he asked me. "That guy thinks he's on *MasterChef*." Then he made us laugh, with his deadpan, brilliant impressions of all the other staff in the café. Next he mocked the tourists who expected London wherever they went. "No, we don't do skinny soy lattes. Milk or no milk—your call. Hey, who's hungry?"

We ate with our fingers straight from the ice-cream tubs: quiches and nearly stale wraps stuffed with olives and feta and roasted peppers. There was half a cheesecake, topped with strawberries—about to turn bad, Dev'd said, but it seemed fine to me. It collapsed into my lap and I had to wipe it off my scrawny white thighs.

Eden was licking her fingers, sticky and sweet, still elegant as a cat.

"I'll leave you to it. I need a swim," I told them.

Liam looked up as I got to my feet. His eyes had a question in them. For a second I thought he was going to come with me. But then Eden reached out and took his hand, and he settled back down on the rug.

I took my time finding the spot. You had to know this place well, where to jump from. If you got it wrong, you could break an ankle on the stone shelves jutting out under the black, peaty water. I checked for thistles, stepping carefully in bare feet through long grass onto the ledge. I looked down at the pool. The water looked like cider in the shallows, turning to oily darkness in the depths. I took a breath and leaped—a blink of thrill, falling through air—then the shock of the cold, feet crunching on gravel and silt. I pushed up and out, spitting out water, that cool, weedy, dank smell. I shook my head, buzzing with the cold, and dived back under the water.

After a few strokes I glanced up at the high bank, at their long bodies entwined on the rug. Liam was lying on Eden, holding her face in his hands. I looked away, squashing down a sudden rush of something sharp and bitter that rose inside me.

I swam on my back, looking up. There was a plane slicing through the blue, leaving a vapor trail. A bird poured out its heart in tumbling notes, and sheep bleated on the high moor. I floated, letting my hair curl out around me.

Surely this was almost happy? Wasn't it enough? It had been a very long time since happy, but surely this was close? I'd kept my promise. This was Eden's summer. I'd been there for her. She would survive: Today was proof.

I drifted, thinking. Weren't we due some good luck? I was finally painting again. I was training for a long race. Sure, it would be school again next month, but I wasn't looking too closely at that, even as it sped nearer. Maybe things were finally back to normal, whatever that was. But I still felt there was a cloud over my happiness. Not full sunshine. What was miss-ing? What did I expect? Maybe that's how it was now. Maybe that was the best I could hope for.

With my ears under the water, I let the bass churn of the waterfall banish every other thought. When I got too cold, I clambered out, nicking my shin on a ledge of rock, teeth chat-tering. I exaggerated it, giving them warning I was getting near. "Brrr, free-zing!" I rubbed myself warm again, hopping on the spot, and finally went over to the rug.

They were sitting now. I'd heard the phrase "joined at the hip," but this was the first time I'd seen it. They were wedged so tightly together it seemed as though they'd grown into a new, combined creature. He had his arm around her tightly and she seemed smaller, wedged into his armpit. She had been crying—the only sign was a slight redness to her eyes, and their blue seemed greener.

Eden, crying?

"You OK?" I tried not to mind she was crying on Liam, not me. I had only seen tears once after Iona died, and that had not been good. But if she was crying now, maybe she was getting better, letting stuff out.

"Crying on Liam Caffrey's shoulder; who'd have thought it?" Her smile was wide and wobbly.

He kissed the top of her head so gently. "You're OK, Eden. You're gonna be OK." But when he looked at me, I saw some-thing less certain in his eyes.

CHAPTER TWENTY-ONE

3:30 p.m.

What a difference a month makes.

I hurry after Liam, down the narrow path. Ferns and nettles lean in, hiding the ground, and I slip and curse, getting stung. Everything turns dark. The clouds are thicker now, gathering close and low. I can't even see Liam.

In the field to my right, there's a farmer on a four-wheeler bike, waving and yelling something. She turns the engine off and shouts, "And take your bloody rubbish with you this time!"

I flee from her fury, but when I get close to the waterfall, I see what she means. The green field and mossy banks are strewn with crushed beer cans, chocolate wrappers, and disposable barbecue grills. Scraps of plastic are tangled in the brambles.

I stare down at the pool and spot a pale thing, turning slowly in the thundering white water.

My heart flips right over like a pancake in my chest.

It's not a body.

It's a plastic bag.

It's not Eden's top.

It's not Eden.

I stand there scanning the river, checking each bank, till I'm sure.

It can't be Eden. My mind will not accept the possibility that Eden could be dead, now or ever. Stopped. The end. Nothing. No. My best friend is too alive. Too everything. She can't just disappear. What happens to all her Eden-ness? What the hell happens to me, without her?

I stare into the leafy shadows, looking for a ghost.

"Eden? Have you gone? Don't leave me. I need you." I whisper it and my words are whipped into the turbulent air above the falls. I imagine my prayer rushing off downstream, past fields and through the woods and into town, under bridges, past the school and the railway . . . I pray it will reach Eden, wherever she is.

When I can move again, I stub my toe on something hard. There's a metal plaque dug into the ground, etched with dark letters. It jogs a memory loose, one I'd forgotten.

. : ! . .

It was years back, our Year Seven English project. We were excited to be out of school, the whole class clustered on this bank, shuffling close. Some of the lads were mucking about, swinging on branches and pretending to fall in.

"Pass the photo round, class. Come on: time to focus!" Barwell yelled at us to simmer down.

I peered at the photo. Black and white, it showed six young men lounging right here, with these bilberry bushes, solemn-faced in Sunday best, as real and as ordinary as me, just before they went off and got killed in a war.

"Right, listen up," Barwell said. "You know the plan. We'll read the Ted Hughes poem now: You each have your line."

It worked too. It was different reading it out here, with the page ruffled by the breeze. As I read my little section, I looked at the place it described. Everyone shut up, to hear their mates and to do their line:

. . . I know
That bilberried bank, that thick tree, that black wall,
Which are there yet and not changed. From where these sit
You hear the water of seven streams fall
To the roarer in the bottom, and through all
The leafy valley a rumoring of air go.
Pictured here, their expressions listen yet,
And still that valley has not changed its sound
Though their faces are four decades under the ground.

Eden got that last bit, the heart of it. The next lines were harder, describing the war and the deaths of those young men, the same lads in the photo, in their smart suits and polished shoes and those stupid straw hats with ribbons around. And we knew, 'cause we'd looked at it, how each lad was different, but all were full of life and swagger as they sat there.

Here. Where we stood.

After the poem, we were quiet. The waterfall sounded very loud. You could hear the wind in the trees.

"Well done," Barwell told us. "Now your words, please. What's he saying, our Ted?"

Charlotte put her hand up. It looked strange—with the sparkling river, not a classroom, behind her. "It's right here. I mean, he's got it right, this exact spot with the trees and the water and stuff."

Billy talked over her, not waiting for permission. "Nah, it's about the soldiers more than anything, in't it, sir? The ones in the picture, right before they got killed."

Someone chipped in with explosive sound effects, but Billy closed them down. "Shut up, idiot."

Eden spoke next, her voice high and clear. "And it's about how you can't imagine being dead, when you're right here, so alive. Those soldiers . . . they were as alive as we are now. But now they're all gone. And the poet's gone."

Barwell was about to step in, but she wasn't finished.

"And we'll all be dead one day too. And you just can't get your head around it. That's what he's saying, isn't he, sir?"

"Exactly. Merit for that, Eden Holby," Barwell said softly. And we all stood there, letting it sink in, listening to the sound of the water flowing endlessly downhill.

. • : • •

"She's not here." Liam speaks from behind me and I nearly slip off the path into the pool.

"Make me jump, why don't you?" I snap at him.

"I thought you'd want to know." He stares at me expressionlessly. "I checked up- and downriver. Clear."

"OK," I sigh, telling myself that this negative can still be a positive. We can tick something off our list. We're one step closer to finding her. "So where do we go from here?" I think aloud. "I guess we might as well use our position, do a sweep downstream." I know these hills well from all the different routes our running coach sets us. "If we do this whole valley, duck down into the crags, and then we can go over the hill to the poet's house. That's where we went on our residential trip."

"So?" Liam's staring past me, up the path we came down, like he's checking that no one is coming.

A shiver goes through me. For the first time, I wonder if he planned it this way. This was his idea. Did he bring me out here on my own for a reason? He was being strange about Eden's diary too. Had she written something that would incriminate him?

I make my voice brisk and practical to sound stronger than I feel. "Stuff happened there. It's worth a try."

"OK."

"Got any better ideas?" I challenge him, keeping on with the brave face.

He shakes his head.

"Well, that's my plan anyway." I get a different feeling around him all of a sudden. It's like a change in the weather. A cloud over the sun. We're not a good team right now. Instead, the hairs on the back of my neck stand up, and I react like a spooked horse, shying away from him.

"Why don't we split up?" I call out, moving away. "We'll cover more ground that way." I put more distance between us. "You choose a different route. Take another path, yeah?" I walk over the little stone bridge. The water slides underneath me, smooth, deep, and syrupy brown, rushing to the falls.

Liam stands on the other bank, watching me. His face is in deep shadow and I can't see his expression.

I turn and go up the rugged tussocky path on the far side of the valley. My heart is beating fast now, from the exertion and something else. I glance over my shoulder.

Liam moves fast too, throwing himself at the hill to catch me.

It's fine, I can outrun him over distance. All I need is a head start. So I push myself, stumbling on the dry churned-up turf.

Behind me, Liam speeds up.

CHAPTER TWENTY-TWO

3:42 p.m.

"Jess, wait!"

I don't wait. I keep my head down and lengthen my stride. I reach the top of the slope and fling myself down the main path. That's when I trip and go flying. I land hard in the sun-dried dirt.

"Didn't you hear me, Jess? I said, wait!" Liam's there. He puts one hand under my elbow and starts helping me up.

"What are you doing?" I shake him off with more force than it needs. His touch is toxic today. It burns me. My palms are on fire too, scraped white skin. Blood takes a moment longer to seep through. My legs are trembling from the adrenaline surge.

"Me?" He looks angry. "You're the one who started sprinting off like a frightened rabbit!"

"Look, we haven't got time to stand here bickering. We need to cover some distance. We need to search properly." I dust myself off—there's little bullets of dried sheep poo clinging to my leggings—and turn away, ready to run again. "We're wasting time!"

"Oh, and that's my fault?" Liam's standing in an old gateway between dry stone walls, only there's no gate, just rusty metal hinges holding thin air. Behind him the dusty track slopes off into the distance, to where hills curve in a dark wooded V with paler green horizon behind.

I don't answer. I don't want to be with him anymore. I can't think straight near him. He pulls my thoughts off course, like a magnet: attracting, repelling.

"You think that, don't you?" He takes my silence for an answer. "You're blaming me, just like the others!" The sun's in his eyes, and his face is all scrunched up.

A switch flicks inside me, and I lose it with him. "Well, you saw her last; you tell me! Something must've happened!"

We're facing off against each other now.

"Yeah, Sherlock," he snaps back. "Something happened—where've you been all summer? And you know full well, with that girl, anything could happen. You know what Eden's like. Up and down like a flippin' yo-yo. She's not exactly stable, your mate."

"Oh, so she's just *my* mate now, is she? See how quick you want to be rid of her." And I hate him suddenly for being able to shrug her off like that. He's known her ten minutes compared to me. She's my best friend, for life. However long that is. "Don't you dare talk about Eden like that!" I'm shouting in his face, so close I see a fleck of my spit land on his cheek.

"Oh, it starts here, does it? Just 'cause she's missing, she's perfect suddenly? You and me know that's so not true."

"Shut your mouth!" I shriek at him.

"And if she's dead, let's make her a saint, like they did with her psycho sister?"

I slap him.

He grabs my hand and hoists me up toward him, hissing in my face. "These your true colors, Jess Mayfield?" His mouth twists in a sour smirk. "What? So violence is only wrong when it's directed against you? When you get to play the little victim?"

I gasp and try to struggle away.

"But you get to lash out any time you like?"

My heart's hammering. The white sky spins above us. Liam's face looms into mine, like a nightmare version of last Saturday night. His blue eyes narrow, sparking pain.

"What if I'd done that to you, and you'd run to the police? What do you think, Jess? You think I'd get sympathy? You girls! All your banging on about *fair* this, *equal* that. You've got no clue. Fair works both ways and you're not playing fair."

I'm lost. My vision's breaking up in a snowstorm of silver dots. His words reach me distantly through the sea of panic.

"I don't do violence—not before Clarkson, and never again. But you do, apparently. Good thing I've found out now, before I got in any deeper. I thought you were the sane one, Jess."

He throws my hand away and I fall back against the grass at the edge of the track. I rub my wrist, hot and sore where he held it, and listen to his footsteps pounding away into the distance.

The worst thing is, he's right about Eden, and it looks like he's right about me too.

CHAPTER TWENTY-THREE

4:16 p.m.

I jog down the valley on the same path as Liam took, past the quiet National Trust's parking lot. I've wiped the blood from my scraped skin on my tunic. Maybe that's why I get weird looks from the weekday dog walkers. I'm trying not to think about what Liam said. I tell myself I'm on autopilot, searching as I fly.

I get to the gateway of the National Trust estate. There's a four-by-four police car parked where the ice cream van usually is, two officers in high-vis jackets waiting by the roadside. They wave down a passing car, and a young male officer leans in to talk to the driver.

I make myself move, on feet that feel like stone. Closer, closer, I strain to hear his words.

"Excuse me, sir, I wonder if . . . *missing teenager* . . . Sixteen years old, blond . . . last seen . . ." He shows the man a photo.

"Did you notice . . . unusual . . . last night . . . this morning?"

The driver's a bald man, middle-aged, in a tweed jacket,

with two black spaniels filling the passenger seat. "No. Not seen nothing." He presses a button to close the window and drives away before the questions are done.

"Thank you for your time, sir," the officer finishes sarcastically as the car accelerates around the corner away from him.

Is that how little Eden matters, if you don't know her? Is she an inconvenience? A delay in your routine, like a traffic jam? Or is he escaping because he does know something? Blink once: He's a nutter; he's got Eden tied up in his barn. Blink twice: He's an ordinary bloke, in a hurry to get home.

"Yes?" The young policeman sees me approaching. I don't get politeness, just the tail end of his frustration.

"What is it? Have you heard anything? I'm her friend. I talked to the police this morning. Your colleagues . . ." I manage to name one of the women I spoke to.

"Nothing to worry about, just following up leads," he says dismissively.

"Leads? What do you mean, leads? Has someone seen her?" Hope flutters its wings in my rib cage.

The young police officer looks down at me. His eyes are light brown. I can see a nick in the black stubble on his cheek where he cut himself shaving. Not much older than me, he treats me like a kid. "We're gathering information as part of the wider investigation." There he goes with the official words, words like locked gates that don't let me in.

"Yeah, but have you heard anything?" My voice is shrill.

He turns his back as another car approaches.

"Hey! I'm talking to you. What leads?"

His female colleague pats my arm. "Listen, love, I know it's hard, but you have to leave us to do our job. We're doing all we can."

I spin and face her. She's got a more open face: warm brown skin, laughter lines around eyes that actually see me. She says, "So you're her friend? Did you have anything new to tell us?"

I shake my head and look at my dusty running shoes.

"Shouldn't you be getting back home, then? Do you want me to ring someone for you?"

Another headshake, and I lie, "It's OK, it's just over there." I wave my hand vaguely toward the southern hillside, where a few cottages huddle on the far side of the river.

"All right, love. Keep an eye on our social media, local radio, and TV. You'll hear when we find her. Take care till then, OK?" Her brow is creased with worry.

I walk away with my shoulders back and my head high, trying to look purposeful. I feel her watching me, but I don't look round.

When I know the police officers can't see me anymore, I break into a jog, pacing myself. I don't know how many miles of this marathon are left. Dodging rocks and roots, I go up the hill, through the woods and over into the next valley, down the steep lane to the writers' center where we came on the residential trip. The sun comes out again: heavy amber bars slanting through the trees. Huge beeches, like giants guarding the entrance gates to the poet's house. Oh, the stuff they've seen: over hundreds of years, in all weathers.

"Have you seen Eden? Where did she go?" I ask the trees as I

slip past. I know I shouldn't be here. The staff will be busy with another group. It's someone else's home this week, not mine. But I can't help feeling—because of what happened here—a little bit of it will always belong to me.

· • ⁝ •· •

After Iona's funeral, I didn't see Eden for weeks. Radio silence. I wondered what was happening up at their house, the three of them where there had been four. A missing limb.

Someone decided the creative-writing residential would be the best way of "easing Eden back into the school context without the stress of her usual class schedule." And when someone dropped out, Barwell offered me the spare place so I could come along with Eden. Me and all the top-track English class. Liam didn't get a look in. We went up there after school on that Monday in the sweaty little school minibus, just a mile or two up the hill and down a steep straight lane: like a chute into another world.

I sat next to Eden on the way. She didn't speak much. I felt shy of her, rusty at being her friend. "Want some Diet Coke? . . . I bought a new notebook and a spare if you need?" Everything I said sounded stupid, stilted, irrelevant. What did you say to a girl who'd just lost her sister?

The bus spat us out next to dark stone buildings that belonged to a different century. In the pouring rain, the place seemed to match the poet who'd once lived here. Beautiful, but kind of forbidding.

I tumbled away from the stew of the minibus. Since last year, I'd hated the rain. It reminded me of *that day*, but this smelled different: fresher. I followed Josh, Imogen, and the others into the grounds: There was an apron of landscaped gardens jutting out over a stunning view. The valley cut a deep wedge between wooded hills, with the town tucked tactfully out of sight around the corner. The only noise was the rushing river far below us.

"I'm king of the world!" Josh yelled into the rain, with his hands in the air, leaning right over the railing. His cronies laughed, but I was with him for once. It felt as if we'd stepped through a portal to a magic kingdom.

"Hey, I'm Rose. Welcome." A smiling woman with purple hair opened a front door that was thicker than my arm. "Come in out of the rain and put your bags in here." She was in her late twenties, with an oval face, a kind smile, and the bluest eyes I'd ever seen. She was wearing a grungy black T-shirt, a lace skirt, and huge hobnailed boots that were even bigger than mine.

I liked her straight away. Even more when I saw the tray of tea and cake she'd laid out before an open fire.

Rose counted us in and served us cake while she explained the rules for the week. Afterward, she showed us our bedrooms. Me and Eden got our very own staircase—like fairy-tale princesses in a tower—leading to two little attic rooms on the second floor.

"Which of you is Jess Mayfield?" Rose read from her crumpled sheet of paper. "You're in here."

I looked through the doorway and my heart clicked its heels. It was a little square room, empty except for a single bed covered in an orange throw, a small table with a bronze lamp, a chest of drawers, and an old wooden desk and chair. The ceiling curved down low under the eaves, held up by dark beams, to a huge window. The view was like a painting: silver rain needling down the valley, steep fields and the woods with their million shades of green. I could even hear the river.

"And you must be Eden? Here." She opened the other door: a smaller room with no windows, only skylights where the rain was tap-dancing loudly. "Not quite the same view, but cozy, right?"

I glanced at Eden's face. "Or can she bring her mattress in here and share with me?" I asked.

"Sure, just let me know," Rose said, smiled, and left.

"What do you think, E?" I said as Rose went back down our stairs. "Do you want to share, or go solitary? Either works for me." I kept it light, trying to hide my concern. She'd gone inside herself, somewhere a long way down, and I didn't know how to follow.

Eden shrugged. "I'll stay put. Not really here for the views." She went in and lay on her bed without closing the door. She put her headphones on and stared up at the rain hammering on the glass.

I waited for a long moment, but I couldn't think of what to say. I went to unpack, taking possession of my room. I loved everything about it. I wondered about all the other people who'd ever slept here. It felt as though I could almost see their shadows, or feel the imprint they'd left behind like dust.

I could hear the others yelling and stampeding along the corridor below. Someone knocked on my door.

Barwell waited, carefully not crossing my threshold. "Everything OK, Jess?"

"Sir." I nodded. "Better than OK. Look at this."

"Lucky you. I'm out in the barn near the boys. Rose is at the end of the corridor, next landing down, if you need her. How's Eden?" he added in a loud whisper.

"Like you'd expect," I told him.

He slumped a bit. "Dinner's in ten. See if you can persuade her to come down?"

Everyone except Eden spent that ten minutes shrieking and chasing each other through the massive echoing rooms, discovering a library lined with bookshelves, several pianos, a whole floor of high-ceilinged bedrooms, and a dining table that could seat all twenty of us, no problem at all.

Barwell looked different here too. He'd changed into jeans and T-shirt instead of his usual suit and tie.

At dinner, Charlotte asked cheekily, "So can we call you Neil this week, sir?"

"No, you flippin' well can't. I'm still your teacher, and I'm in loco parentis. You know what that means?"

"Nah."

"For this week only, I'm your mum and your dad rolled into one: *über-dad*," he growled in a stupid voice. "So you'd better do as I say!" But he twinkled into his mug of tea. "Anyway, I'm not teaching today. The writers here are in charge." He gestured at the other adults, helping themselves to baked potatoes and beans, right along with us.

There was a tall, softly spoken children's author called Tom. He had a gray beard, a stoop, and a dry sense of humor, and soon seemed like everyone's favorite uncle. He had a line of bruises across his forehead—the doorways were brutally low here.

And there was a poet called Aisha, not five years older than us, but already published and so confident that she shone. She talked easily about rhyme and imagery, throwing magic words into the air like juggling balls.

Straight after dinner, Aisha held the first workshop of the week. "OK, we launch in here, people. Icebreaker, word maker, dive in now. No passes out. Everyone reads. They're my rules, right? Work in pairs for my lucky draw. Pick a card from this bag and describe each other, using only the clue you chose."

Eden was as absent as it was possible to be in a room full of twenty people all squashed in around the fire on four different sofas.

I grabbed a card and read it out to her. "'Food or drink.' Sounds all right. You go first?"

She blinked at me, pale and vacant.

"Come on, what would Josh say you were?" I whispered, glancing over to where Josh was telling his mate Danny that, no, he couldn't be a Porsche, he wasn't that fine.

"He'd say I was coffee," Eden said finally, in a low, hoarse voice. "He thinks I'm strong, addictive, dark, all that stuff."

"Nah, you'd be tea, not coffee," I said, relieved to hear her speak.

"What, milky and boring? Ta very much!" She didn't smile, but it was only a moment away, if I kept on trying.

"Eden Holby, how many cups of tea do I drink every single day of my life?" I lifted the mug at my feet to make my point.

"Ten? Fifteen?"

"Exactly. Don't bash the brew, E. I love my tea. Tea rocks. But if you like, you can be a posh one: Lady Grey?"

"OK, I'll take that; cheers."

Her lips finally curved into a brief, trembling smile.

I high-fived myself on the inside. "What am I, then, E? Make it good! I'm thinking champagne . . . hot chocolate at the very least . . ."

"Ah, easy. You're a glass of water, J."

"What's that—plain, cheap, and everyday?" I teased, keeping it warm and light.

"No, I can't survive long without it."

I looked over. She met my gaze with eyes that shone. I leaned in and hugged her hard, burying my face in her apple-scented hair. I heard the conversations around us quieten, felt the weight of eyes on our backs. I didn't care. I'd be her safety barrier. I'd stand between Eden and the world.

CHAPTER TWENTY-FOUR

Next morning around the dining table gleaming in the muted morning light, Aisha read us a poem by Ted Hughes.

This house has been far out at sea all night,
The woods crashing through darkness, the booming hills,
Winds stampeding the fields under the window
Floundering black astride and blinding wet

Till day rose . . .

It was about this actual house, by that actual poet who'd lived here, the one staring down at us from a photo on the wall with the startled, hunted look in his eyes. "What do you think?" Aisha asked.

Silence.

"Look, this is your territory. This is right here!"

I think she meant it as inspiration. It didn't work like that. His strong, supple words left me speechless. He'd been here first. He said it all. He said it too well. And if not him, his first brilliant wife, who'd killed herself. Between them, they had all the angles covered when it came to this valley.

I tried to say it. "Yeah, but, miss?"

"I've told you—Jess, isn't it?—call me Aisha. I'm not your teacher and we're not at school."

"Aisha, then. I mean, they've not left any space for us, have they? If we talk about the moors, it's all Cathy and Heathcliff." I gestured at the portrait of Ted Hughes. "If we talk about this house, or this weather, we're copying him. If we talk about depression and that"—I ignored all the faces that turned to Eden now, like a shoal of fish—"then Sylvia got there first. It's all been said."

Aisha sighed. "OK. Who else thinks this?"

A few hands went up.

"You know what? Some people say there are only seven stories in the world. Seven! All the others are variations on those. But if I asked you now to write me a story about the worst experience of your life, I'd get sixteen different stories. And none of them would be boring. Am I right?"

Mutters of agreement.

"There might be seven stories, but there are a billion ways of telling them. So—thanks, Jess—this is today's assignment. I want you to write a short *fictionalized* version of something either very good or very bad that has happened to you. Remember, that's short—a page or two. And that's fiction—no real people, people! OK?"

I did it too. When Eden fell asleep after lunch, I took a chair into her room and watched over her. While she slept, I got out my sketchbook. I didn't mean to, but I started drawing properly—not just tattoo designs—for the first time since last November. And it flowed out, like it was all there, and I was just the printer spewing page after page.

Later that evening I copied it out and went to find Aisha. "Miss? Aisha, I mean. Here's mine." I thrust it at her as if it might bite me if I held on to it too long.

"Thank you, Jess." She didn't look at it then and I was glad. "Make an appointment for tomorrow, after lunch. We'll talk about it then."

The next day, I was surprised how nervous I was. All morning, each time I remembered the appointment, something lurched inside me. Finally, after I'd eaten about half a bowl of soup and chased some salad around my plate for a bit, it was time.

My name was the first on the sign-up sheet pinned to the door of the library. *2:30 Jess Mayfield.* I knocked on the white painted wood. You could see where the brushstrokes had been, where they'd left little beads of paint.

"Come in, Jess."

I went in. A posh house's grand personal library, like you might see in a film, with a deep red carpet. The walls were lined with books, except for one wall that was mainly window, and another that was filled by a massive stone fireplace with a big black stove in it. It smelled old but nice in here: like wood and polish, paper and ash. Aisha was sitting at the long table, but her back was to the window, so it was hard to see her expression. There was a thick shaft of sunlight with tiny gold specks floating through it like fairy dust.

I sat down and fumbled for a pen and paper, in case I was supposed to write anything down. I noticed she had my pages in front of her and my mouth went dry.

"Jess? So this is based on my challenge, right? This story is a bit like something that happened?"

I nodded. I couldn't look at her now, so I concentrated on my fingers, which were trembling. I slapped the pen down, spreading my fingers on the desk to stop the shakes.

"This is it." Aisha's voice changed, so that I couldn't help sneaking a quick look. She was blinking fast. She cleared her throat. "This is how you speak of the unspeakable. This is how you speak even when others have come first and told their stories so strongly. This is how, Jess. In your words. In your way. No one else in the world could've created this. Do you see? This is it."

Inside me, the thaw quickened. I heard the *flump* of falling snow, the drip of icicles, faster, faster, faster, and the rush of meltwater.

"There's not many words," I mumbled.

"Yeah, but—Jess?—they're the right ones."

I tried to tell her. "I couldn't draw, afterward . . ."

"You can certainly draw now. And, Jess, you have to do this. When it's time to choose what you do next, please, will you remember what I said? You have a real talent. For art, sure—you must already know that. But also for this, words and pictures on a page that are unique and powerful. I don't have any other feedback for you. This is just right. The shape, the content. What you left out. What you put in. You made me cry, and I can promise you, I don't say that often."

She stood up then, and I mirrored her. She came around the table and paused with one hand on the door handle, ready to open it for me. She kept a distance between us, but now that she was facing the light, I got the full beam of her smile and the look in those tiger eyes and it was better than a hug. "I wish you all the luck in the world, you brave woman."

I went outside. I didn't know what to do. I wanted to hold the feeling a bit longer before I spoke to anyone. I went out and wandered around the house in a daze. I sleepwalked down through the gardens below. There was a bench there, looking out across the whole valley. I saw no one. I sat down with my bag and my papers held tight against me and I felt the warm afternoon sun on my face. I watched the rabbits hop and graze in the steep fields. A herd of white cows, chewing. The air was full of motion, the churn of the river and the trees, swaying green, but I sat completely still, smiling.

CHAPTER TWENTY-FIVE

On the last night of the residential, there was this grand finale.
A showcase of our talent. We gathered in the converted barn.
Spotlights angled from high beams above us, making a circle of
light that was our stage. We sat on squishy sofas, not slumped
as on previous evenings, but alert and twittering with nerves.
All day people had stressed about this, rehearsing lines, editing
poems—you'd think it was a big deal. Maybe it was. Maybe it
was a beginning.

I was in the middle and Eden's name came last in the hand-
drawn running order pinned to the whiteboard. Mr. Barwell sat
on the edge of his seat, sucking it up. Rose had her camera out.
Tom and Aisha were glowing and proud. They launched us, with
words like: *did yourselves proud . . . transformed . . . inner voice . . .
you are writers now.*

One by one, people stood and shared their work. Blushing,
stammering, or defiant. Imogen filled three tissues reading a

poem about her late granddad. Charlotte read a sonnet about a friend's eating disorder. Danny did a funny short story about getting lost in a video game. And Josh glanced meaningfully from under his floppy bangs while he read a haiku, making everyone stare at Eden.

She looked down at her clasped hands the whole time, only uncurling to clap for each person.

Finally, it was me. I walked out, under the bright lights. I'd taken care with my makeup: the full works tonight. I had my hair twisted up, with a scarf around the scar, a few red plaits falling loose, my favorite lace-and-velvet black dress, and my old boots. I found a spot on the polished wooden boards. I looked at my audience. My body tried its best to pull the usual tricks: palms sweaty, throat dry, legs wobbling. I ignored it. Tonight, I was the boss. I knew I couldn't read the strip I'd done for Aisha, so I went for the easy win. It wasn't a great poem, but it summed up our week. I cleared my throat and began.

I'm Brontë'd out. I'm over Heathcliff.
I'm even done with Plath and Hughes.
I'm stumbling, tripping, till I see
I cannot walk in dead poets' shoes.

I need to talk of a hawk
—In sun, snow, or rain—
I need to walk in these hills
Until they're mine again.

I wanna get Gothic, do some wuthering,
Set fire to my attic, get lost on the moor.
But everywhere I turn, all the words are gone.
How do I speak, when they got there before?

I'll speak 'cause I have to.
I'll speak in this tongue
'Cause it's this place that made me
And it's here that I run.

I wasn't prepared for the amount of applause I got, the stamping feet and the whoops. My wobbles vanished. My thaw turned to summertime under Aisha's dazzling grin. I smiled and bowed and returned to my seat, letting waves of elation lap over me.

"Go, Jess!" Eden whispered, giving my arm a squeeze.

When it was her turn, Eden stood a little unsteadily. She walked out to the front, gripping her piece of paper. She was wearing a red-checked shirt, open over a tight black camisole. Her denim skirt was micro-short, but she'd made it slouchy with leggings and boots. Her hair looked greasy, not like her at all. She squinted against the glare of the lights, and began.

It was the best thing anyone had written all week—you could see it from the shocked expressions on the adults' faces. Eden's voice was brittle and knowing, mocking her own pain. And maybe she was channeling the American poet, the one who was buried here, stuck for eternity in this crooked little village on the top of a rain-swept hill.

The celebratory mood vanished. Imo started crying again.

Eden finished with a flourish, imitating Aisha. She put her paper away and spat every word at us, in case we missed her meaning:

> . . . *haunted by a lipsticked shade.*
> *You seek revenge, you do.*
> *Just the subtle blade*
> *Of sharpened guilt, to send me*
> *Headlong after you—*

She stopped, mouth open, midline.

Her face seemed to elongate, till it looked like that famous painting, the awful scream. Only no more noise came. Instead, she froze there for a long moment, and then fled, her boots thudding on the wooden stairs.

I shot from my seat.

I heard Barwell barking, "Right, you lot! Stay here with Tom and Aisha—OK?" Steps drummed after me.

Outside was still and quiet, no sign of Eden. I ran for the house. "I'll take upstairs, sir. You look down here." I checked Eden's room, then mine. I did a quick sweep of the first floor, slamming each door open. Bathrooms. Nothing. "Eden! *Eden!*" I threw myself downstairs. Three steps at a time. Nearly collided with Barwell and we both ran out through the back door.

Rose was outside on the terraced lawn, scanning up and down the valley. It was barely dark and the rain had stopped. The sky was darkening blue, a paler smudge over the horizon.

Rose cupped her hands and yelled, "Eden!" so loud it bounced back at us with a faint mocking echo.

Barwell started losing it. "No, no, no. Not Eden. Not now. Shit, shit, shit."

"Neil?" Rose was the together one. "Get a grip. Let's think. What's your guess?"

"You don't get it, Rose. Her sister was killed just last month. If anything happens to her . . . Why did I think this would be a good idea? Damn it all."

Rose ignored his panic. "If we get the car out, we can be after her in two minutes. Where would she go, Jess? Home?"

"No." I was sure of it. I leaned on the railing and peered down the valley, at the steeply sloping fields that led down to the river, at the woods beyond. "Shh! Listen? What's that?"

"Just owls," Rose said. "Come on, we've not got long. Have you tried her phone, Jess?"

"Course."

"I don't believe it. This cannot be happening." Barwell was pacing up and down behind us. "What am I going to tell her parents? The headmaster?"

Barwell's fear was contagious. My heart was speeding, my head spinning, still struggling to make the switch from elation to whatever this was. Eden had pulled the carpet from under us, all right, but I didn't know what it meant yet. I kept searching, staring into the darkness, the dense black shadows under the trees.

"Let's split up," Rose was saying. "I'll take the car up to the village. . . . Tom and Aisha will stay here—"

Then I saw her. Down at the bottom of the hill, moving fast, her bright hair still visible, a faint glimmer in the gloom. "There!"

"Jess's right, there she is. By the river. Shit." Barwell was already off, shouting over his shoulder, "Rose, stay here. I've got my phone. I'll call if I need backup. She's had a tough time, this one. Handle with care."

"Here, take my flashlight." Rose passed it to me. "Ring me, OK?" she called after us. "Or I'll follow in ten."

We rushed downhill in the narrow white glare of the flashlight. The steep track was rutted. I heard Barwell trip once, but we threw ourselves onward. I was praying Eden wouldn't disappear into the woods: We'd never find her then.

The path ended with one last hairpin, turning flat and cobbled as it led to a small curved bridge. With all the rain this past week, the river was swollen and fierce, thunderingly loud.

Eden sat on the narrow rim of the bridge, her feet dangling over a ten-foot drop. Below her, I could just make out a torrent of white, hurling itself into the darkness below.

"Not the bridge," Barwell whispered. "What's she playing at?"

I froze. I yanked at Mr. Barwell's sweatshirt to stop him. If we startled her, she might slip.

"Eden!" I called gently. The sound was scrambled by the noise of the falls.

"Eden, it's Mr. Barwell. I've come to fetch you, OK?" His voice was strong and deep. "We'll go back up to the house and talk, all right?"

We crept slowly toward her. Step, pause, step: like cats stalking prey.

Without looking round, she started talking. "Why me?"

I could barely hear her. We went closer in.

"Why does all the worst stuff happen 'cause of me?" She raised her voice now. "I'm the kiss of death, and I've had enough of it. Of hurting people. If it's all a test, y'know what? I've got my results. I admit it: I fail!"

"No!" I called. "You didn't fail! You saved me. Stop it." I peered over the bridge, but it was just roaring darkness.

"Eden!" Barwell shouted. "Eden, come away from there. We're here. We can just sit and talk, OK?"

"I fail!" she yelled into the damp air, full of noise. "I can't do it. I messed up. Again."

"You didn't mess up. Come on," I shouted, scared. I turned to Barwell and hissed, "What do we do?"

"Take it slow," he answered me from the side of his mouth. "Don't startle her, OK?" The flashlight's glare wobbled. "Eden, please, turn round, come off the bridge, yeah?" His voice was showing the strain now.

"Why?" Eden said over her shoulder, quite calm.

"Come over here; we can talk." Barwell seemed paralyzed. He turned into a flashlight-bearing statue, five paces back.

"Talk? I'm sick of talking. I'm even sick of drinking—doesn't bloody work anymore."

That's when I realized she was drunk. Why hadn't I thought of that? The afternoon naps, the morning grogginess—I'd put everything down to fresh grief.

I felt a bitter rush of irritation, along with the fear. We didn't have to be here. We could be sitting in the barn, feeling a warm glow, applauding the others. "Flipping heck. She's just drunk. Not suicidal." I turned brisk, impatient. "We talk her down, get her back up the hill, it'll be fine. Right, sir?" Part of me was ready to do whatever it took to fix this and help Eden; another part was pouting and sulking inside me. Why did she have to do this? This was supposed to be a good week. Time out in this lovely place. I was getting better, she was getting better. It was all working out, till now. But she could lose her balance and slip off the bridge before I could even reach her, so I had to take it seriously. I kept moving, biting down the urge to scream at her. *Drama queen, get off the bloody bridge.*

"I'm sick of plodding on." Her voice was slightly slurring.

Yeah, I'm sick of it too, but that's life. I was almost there. Slowly, slowly, I reached out and touched her shoulder, then passed my arm gently across her front, turning her gradually toward me, praying I had her weight. "Come on. Come off there. We can talk better down here, OK?"

She was passive now, letting me steer her. "Sick of waiting for it to get better. Sick of everyone pretending. Sick of *sympathy*. Sick of my parents," she mumbled through her list. "Sick of my own head. It's not pretty in there, no, sirree."

"Hey, it's all right." I had her. "Come here." This wasn't our way, but I'd have to take charge. I'd lead, and she'd bloody well have to follow, just for a bit.

I tugged at her left leg, nudged it off the bridge onto the ground, then the other, so she was facing inward again.

She wouldn't look at me. Her hair was loose, covering her face. She collapsed forward, limp as a rag doll, onto the gravelly path.

"It's me, Eden. I don't mind what your head's like. We can sort it out." I slid down next to her, leaning on the stone of the bridge, supporting her into a sitting position. "You and me, we always do."

"S'too late now. This is bigger'n me."

"You listen to me, Eden Holby." I was babbling, as if my words could drown out her pain and my resentment. I owed it to her, so I said the right thing and ignored my inner tantrum. "It's bound to be tough, and I know I haven't been there. I'm sorry. You've gotta let me help, OK?"

"You've had an extraordinarily difficult time." Barwell chipped in with the official version, still not daring to get too close, as if we were made of fine china. Or dynamite. "But things won't always be this bad."

"Eden, I was giving you space." I told her the truth: "Then I was trying to help. I'm sorry if it's not been enough." I had tears in my eyes now, tears for her and for me, blurring my vision. "I mean, I know it's not enough." I'd wanted to save her. I'd been in love with that idea this week, I saw now. Who did I think I was, her knight in shining armor? *Don't worry, Eden! Your sister may be dead, but you still have me!* I wouldn't even have come on the residential if Barwell hadn't asked me to look after her. This wasn't about me. It was about Eden.

My fingers gripped her wrist, her warm skin, and finally it seemed to reach her.

"No, Jess. You're enough. It's not that. I'm sorry." She looked over at Mr. Barwell. "Sorry, sir. I shouldn't have run out. Didn't mean to spoil it. Just . . . jus . . ."

Barwell crouched on his heels, watching, as she ran out of speech. He dared to come closer now.

Her face stretched in a horrible grimace and she let out a high-pitched wail, pure pain. I caught the scent of alcohol on her breath: She must have been drinking all day in her room. She started sobbing and rocking, holding her chest.

"Shhh. It's OK, it's going to be OK." I grabbed her from the side, clutching her to me. My resentment evaporated, replaced by guilt.

She snorted, a deep, snotty grunt that turned into a choking cough. "Well, that shows what you know. It is all my fault. Iona died 'cause of me." It all came out in a hiccupping confession. "We fought that night. Mum and Dad tried to stop us. I was miserable and I took it out on her. I wanted her to feel as bad as me. I said some vicious things. When she got in the car, she was furious. She was crying."

"B-b-but the police report said it wasn't her fault," I stammered.

"No,"—Barwell joined in—"the other car was speeding. It came around the bend on her side. There was nothing she could do. . . ."

"Ever tried driving when you're in tears? There's probably a law against it." She laughed and put on a stupid, serious voice: "No driving under the influence of alcohol, drugs, or blinding tears."

"Eden Holby, you listen to me," I said. "Your sister died in an awful accident. Accident! That means it's not your fault."

"It is, Jess. It's completely my fault. Just like you getting attacked was my fault. I made you come out in the rain. I made Iona run off that night. I'm cursed, and it's got to stop."

"That driver—the one who killed Iona—he paid with his life. Don't think you have to pay for it too. This is hard enough without blaming yourself." Barwell's voice was deep and gentle, but snagging on tears. "You have to listen to me: Let this go. Nobody thinks it's your fault."

"My parents do." She raised her head briefly. Her mascara was smeared around her eyes, and her cheeks were slimy and damp in the beam of the flashlight. "If it wasn't for me and the things I said, Iona would not have been in that car, going around that corner at that moment."

"I can assure you they don't. They love you. They're worried about you." Barwell finally came and sat next to us on the damp ground, the three of us in a row, leaning on the bridge. "Think about them for a second. If you'd fallen in just now and I had to ring them and say you'd been in an accident, it would destroy them. They'd have lost everything. Can you imagine that?"

"Yeah," she said, teeth chattering, seeming to lose steam. "I can imagine that just fine."

I saw Barwell take it like a slap. He swore under his breath. "I'm sorry, Eden. I know I can't imagine what you're dealing with. But please, keep going. It won't always be so hard."

"We'll get through it," I told Eden. I put my head on her

shoulder and waited. "And I'm here for you. Anything you need. It will get better, I promise."

There was a long gap then, but I felt something change.

When she spoke again, she seemed calmer, more sober, and it was almost worse. "Will it get better?" she asked hoarsely. "When? I really hope it's soon, because I'm not sure how much I've got left."

CHAPTER TWENTY-SIX

5:33 p.m.

I shake my head to clear it of these memories. I go through the gateway of the writers' center, feeling as though I am trespassing. I walk into the walled courtyard and grind to a halt, like I'm out of fuel. The dark stone of the poet's house hums with life. There's steam coming from a vent in the kitchen. I hear voices and laughter. Someone is playing a piano. I'm about to retreat, when the door opens and I see a familiar figure coming out, carrying a tray of mugs.

"Rose!"

She turns. "Jess! It is Jess, isn't it?"

For a moment I'm surprised she remembers me. Then I realize: It's not every week that one of her visitors flees to the river in the middle of the last-night reading.

But I'm wrong. That's not the only reason she knows.

"I'm so sorry. I saw the alert online, about Eden. Listen, go wait for me in the garden. We can talk. I'll just deliver these teas."

I walk through the empty garden and look out over the valley. The sun's low and golden, wrapping itself in light scarves of cloud. You can see the first tint of orange in the wooded hills. It'll be autumn soon. Behind me, the front of the house is covered in a vine with bright red leaves, like splashes of blood in the sinking sun.

"Here." Rose comes and hands me a mug of tea. "I'm sorry, Jess. What a horrible day for you."

"Thanks." I take a sip. The tea tastes weird and floury—soy milk, maybe?—but it's hot and comforting. "So you saw the stuff about Eden we posted online?"

"Yep. Shared it too." She turns to face me. "They'll find her." Her blue eyes are calm and steady.

"I've been looking all day. Sorry, I don't even know why I'm here, except I'm retracing our steps, from this summer, and I just thought . . . I know I shouldn't be here."

"It's all right. It was worth asking. But we've not seen Eden. I'd have rung the police if I had."

I am very tired all of a sudden. Rose is being so kind, but it only makes me want to cry. "Can I sit down?" I back away blurrily for the bench against the front of the house. I put my head back against the stone and close my eyes to hide tears.

"When did you last eat?"

I shrug.

"Stay there. I'll bring you something."

I try to get a grip while she's gone, letting the sun warm me, sipping my tea. It'll be dark soon, and then it all gets harder.

I imagine looking for Eden in the night, in the rain. I'll never stop looking for her.

Rose's voice pulls me from that grim vision. "Jess?" She's holding out a plate piled with food.

"Oh. I . . . I . . . I mean, thank you."

"It's fine, it's just leftovers. You feeling any better?"

I nod.

"Listen, I have to go. They need me inside. It's their Friday-night showcase—remember that? Stay a while; eat that and leave the plate there when you're done. I'm working till eleven, but I'm here if you need help later, OK?"

I'm ridiculously grateful, but she's gone before I can find the words to say it. The plate is crammed with some kind of cheese pastry, potatoes, and a grainy salad with beans and peppers. I eat it all fast, glad there's no one to see, and lick my fingers afterward. I go in and use the bathroom at the back of the barn, and then I'm off, out through the gates and away down the rough track to the river.

I pause there, looking over the bridge, reliving that last time. The river is tame today—a kitten, not a lion—but the rocks look worse uncovered. They are slick and black, raw and as sharp as teeth. If Eden had fallen, back then, they were waiting.

The last of the sunlight filters down through the leaves, deep bronze. It catches the fine spray, making a halo, then a rainbow, across the gorge.

My phone buzzes in my pocket. It's Mum. I can't keep ignoring her. Plus, there's a chance by now she's got good news. I tap to accept. "Hi, Mum," I say. "Any news?"

"Oh my God, finally! Didn't you hear me ringing? I've left five messages, Jess. Five! What the hell were you thinking?"

To be honest, I'd stopped counting after three. I hold the phone away from my ear a little.

"Where are you? Are you all right? I've had the school on the phone. What was I supposed to say, that I didn't know where *my* daughter was, *either?*"

She is livid. Force-ten gale. "Mum, I'm OK. I told you, I need to look for Eden. And I'm fine. I can look after myself now, really. I'm up the ravine, on the bridge. I was going to head past her old house next—"

"What are you doing there? You can't just wander the hills—"

"Have you heard anything?" I cut in, ignoring her.

She sighs and I hear the anger draining away as she gears up to tell me something. "There's no official news, just that . . ."

I can hear the effort she's making to control her voice now. My heart flutters, a moth against a flame, drawn to what will end it. "Tell me!"

"It's been on the news, local and national. There're TV vans in town. Poor Claire and Simon. It's bad enough without the media spotlight—"

"What? What are they saying?"

"Oh, love, I'm sorry. I don't even know if it's true. I mean, how could they know—unless the police leaked it or someone's phone was tapped. These days, anything could happen—"

"Mum!" I snap. "Know *what's* true?"

"It's the text, the one Eden sent this morning. They think it was a kind of . . ."

"Yes?" Finally! The truth about the text. About time.

"A kind of suicide note—apologizing to her parents—" Mum's voice breaks off and I can hear her fighting tears. "And the same sort of thing in her diary . . ."

"No. She can't have. She wouldn't. It wasn't, Mum, I know it." I hang on to what I'm saying, willing it to be true, denying any other possibility. But I've still got that diary lock in my pocket, and it begs to differ.

"I know, Jess, I know. But maybe we should prepare ourselves—"

"No! I'm not giving up. How can you even say that?"

"Jess, I promise you, I'm not giving up." Her voice is stronger now, on safer ground. "They're organizing search teams, alongside the police. Coordinating volunteers down at the town hall. I'm going there now. Come and meet me?"

I hesitate. Half of me wants to go, to be part of something bigger than me, to stop making decisions. To be near Mum, to let her look after me.

I look up the valley, at the cascading river and the shadowy paths. I see someone, just upstream, in a blue T-shirt and jeans.

Liam. Coming for me.

"I'll meet you later, OK? There's something I need to do first. I'll keep my phone on."

"Jess? No! Don't you hang up on me. *Jess!*"

I end the call. I'll deal with the consequences later. There will be hell to pay, and I'll pay it gladly, once Eden's back. Till then, everything else can wait.

There's something else that bothers me. Mum's angry, sure, but she's not as worried for me, not like she was this morning. She doesn't think anyone else hurt Eden. She's not frantic about a random nutter stalking teenage girls. She thinks Eden did this to herself. She thinks Eden's gone.

She isn't gone. She isn't! But I remember Eden's face when she saw the tarot cards, as if she was cursed. As if this was her fate, her punishment or something. What if she made it come true, just by believing it? What do they call it? A self-fulfilling prophecy.

I stand there, feeling very cold, waiting for Liam to reach me. The sun has gone behind the hill. I hold on to the cool stone of the bridge, watching the water rushing away from me, taking away my hope.

He gets close. He looks like himself again. Some of the weight has gone from his shoulders. His face is softer. "I'm sorry about before . . ." Then he sees me properly. "What is it, Jess? What did they say?"

And I can't help it. I can't hold it in. The tears come hot and fast.

"I didn't . . . I can't . . . I don't know where she is. They think Eden hurt herself. That her last text was saying good-bye." I'm twisting away from him, trying to escape it, but it's the truth and I can't. Through my tears I tell him, "Liam, we let her down. I can't say sorry. I can't find her and I don't know what to do. . . ." Then there's no more talking from me. The sobs come from somewhere very deep down. They make my shoulders and rib cage shake. They hurt. They fold me over and crumple me up like a piece of scrap paper.

Liam catches my hand. He holds me, all creased up and crying against him. He draws me in close and we sink together. We fall on the dusty ground, right there on the bridge. I feel his hands on my hair, on my back, on my face. And it doesn't feel wrong. It feels right. It feels like home. It feels like the only thing I have left.

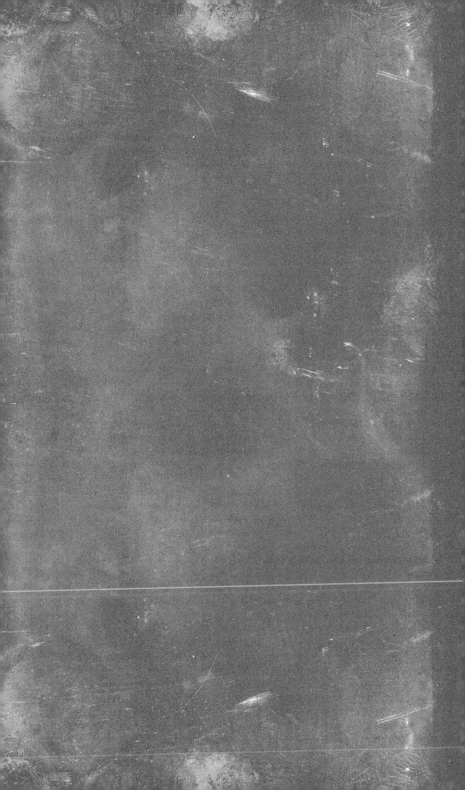

PART THREE

CHAPTER
TWENTY-SEVEN

6:25 p.m.

We pull apart from our collapsed hug. I'm exhausted from the crying. I crawl over to lean against the bridge. We sit there in the gathering dusk, with the river's endless song filling the silence between us. My leg rests against his and it anchors me again.

Eventually, I start telling Liam about that Friday on the residential. About me, Barwell, Eden, right here on this bridge. "If me and Barwell hadn't got there, who knows? She was messed up. Drunk. Guilty. Blaming herself for the accident and the attack."

"But you did get there. And she was OK, for a bit. We were there for her, weren't we?" Liam sounds like he needs convincing. "Even when she pushed us away."

"I should've been able to help her, like she helped me," I say, still damp and hot and full of self-blame. "But what if we didn't? What if we weren't enough? How can I live with myself if . . ." I can't say it. I can't utter the words *she's dead*, in case it makes it true. "And after what we did . . ."

"I know," Liam says. "I feel the same. I feel like such a . . ." He swears. "I was supposed to be her boyfriend. Great job I made of that."

"It's not your fault." It's so much easier to say that about someone else. "We're all in it together. It's like, like . . . when climbers get roped together." I picture the three of us: me, Eden, Liam, knotted together on an icy rock face, with a blizzard blowing around us.

"What? She falls, we all fall? Nice one, Jess."

"No! She falls and we stop her, pull her up—isn't that the point of the rope? I just hope I'm bloody strong enough, 'cause otherwise we're all going down." And somewhere deep down, I know it's true. We need to save Eden 'cause we love her. But also because saving her is the only thing that can save us.

He doesn't reply.

"I'm sorry. For the slap. Just for the record: I don't do that. And I don't think it's OK—"

"Jess, it's all right. I know that. It's not exactly a normal day." He turns to me in the fading light and gives me a quick flash of something like a smile. "What a mess."

I wonder what it'd be like—me and him—without any of this crap going on. But it's not like we exist, perfect pure versions of ourselves, off in a laboratory somewhere. I can't separate how I feel for him from how I feel for Eden or how he feels about Eden. It's tangled up together. So tangled, so messy; I don't know how to sort out the knots without hurting someone.

"We've got to keep looking. Where do we go now?" He

checks his phone: Its display lights up the gloom. "They'll be setting up that full-moon party. Dark soon. How about we go that way, have a look there—then back to town, join the official search?"

I shrug. "I was going to check the river near her old house. They loved it there. It was Iona's favorite. . . . But yeah, we're running out of time. Let's do your plan." It's the best one we've got—it's even got two parts—and I text Mum, to let her know.

. • ⦂ • ·

We turn up the valley and take well-worn footpaths under the trees. We're not the only ones. Soon the darkening woods are full of shadows, flashlight beams, and laughter, people carrying rugs, bags clinking with bottles. Any other night, this would be perfect.

I check my phone again. There's five hours left of the twenty-four since she was last seen. I know that the longer it goes on, the less chance there is of finding her.

Eden? Eden? Can you hear me? Come back. Come back to us. To your parents. To Liam. Or to Tyler. To me. No one will care where you've been or what you've done. As long as you're OK.

We walk single file and Liam must find it easier to talk that way. "Jess, about last Saturday . . . ," he starts, speaking over his shoulder.

Straight for the killer subject. "Uh-huh?" I manage to mumble over the pounding of my heart.

"I know the timing's all wrong. I know it. And I know what it looks like, that I can't be trusted . . ."

That applies to me too, but he doesn't seem to have noticed that.

"But it's not like that. I mean, you've always been there, but I didn't see you till now. Not properly. And yeah, I was flattered when Eden asked me out. I mean, Eden Holby—who wouldn't be?"

The full moon has risen over the hill. Fat and yellow. Harvest moon. The valley transforms in the leafy magical half-light.

I hurry after Liam so I won't miss a word.

"And it was good for a bit. We had fun. But I'd already decided to stop it, back in May. 'Cause we don't really get each other, not really. She's always pushing it. Eden doesn't hear me. She'd never admit it in a million years, but deep down, she thinks I'm not the same as her, not as good."

"No, she doesn't," I tell him. "That's all in your head."

"Even if it is! Still doesn't work, does it?"

"Were you really going to finish it?"

He's stopped. We stand in the middle of a grove of beech trees, tall and massive, making it feel like a church or something.

"Yeah, the day of that parade, back in May. Only all that stuff kicked off. So I couldn't. And then it was June, and, well, you know the rest. After Iona died, it's like I was stuck. And I'm not a total arse—I did want to look after Eden. But I started to see you. Really see you, Jess. That was the only good thing, this summer, getting close to you. Couldn't you tell?"

"Oh, good, I'm glad my best friend's worst nightmare was useful to you! Bloody hell, is that supposed to be flattering? Will you hear yourself?"

The breeze rustles the leaves and I hear an owl ask, "*Who-who?*" so loud it has to be in the next tree.

"Stop it, Jess. I'm just trying to be honest. Can't we keep on wi' that at least?" He sighs.

I know I haven't been honest, with him or with Eden, all summer long. I meet Liam's eyes properly. Even frowning—his dark brows telling me he means it—he's so beautiful it makes me catch my breath. The way he's looking at me in the silvery light does something to my body that I feel all the way down to my toes, like an electric shock that goes right through me.

The ferns shiver and I catch movement above us. The owl launches, wide wings, and floats down the valley like a ghost, leaving us.

"What really happened then, the day of the parade?" I ask. It's not my most pressing question, but it'll keep him talking about Eden—not about us—while we walk up the valley.

CHAPTER TWENTY-EIGHT

7:21 p.m.

"She didn't tell you? About her and Iona fighting?"

"Sure. I mean, I knew it was bad," I say. The last few weeks before Iona died, their fights had been hideous, I knew that. "The whole school knew it. Eden hated that, being gossiped about."

"That was the worst I'd seen, parade day . . ." He starts walking again but slower now, waiting for me to keep pace on the narrow path.

"Tell me everything," I say. I was away at my dad's, so I missed the parade for the first time in years. "Tell me why it kicked off." Maybe there'll be something in it that can help us now.

"You know how excited she was, right? She'd been practicing on her stilts for weeks."

"I know. And she got one of the best costumes. She was so pleased to be a phoenix rising, not a penguin or something lame."

The Parade We Made happened every year: a sign of early summer, like the clocks changing. Artists had it all designed and they showed you what to do. They made massive sculptures—the showstoppers—eerie, beautiful, unforgettable artworks as big as a house. For just a few pounds, you got to join in and make your own little costume: magic conjured from recycled plastic, paint, and shiny paper.

"She did good," Liam says. "The rain stopped just in time. Her crew led the parade. Streets were packed; there were drummers, bands, the lot. She'd got really good on the stilts, so she was dancing along. She looked amazing."

Ouch. *So I'm jealous now that Eden's boyfriend thinks she's gorgeous? Get a grip, Jess.*

"She was buzzing, laughing, striding forward. Till Iona found her, just before the park. Iona and Katie were sitting on the wall, drinking. I was walking next to Eden. Didn't have a costume, but she gave me one of the flames off her stilts and I just waved it about and kept time with her."

I walk slowly and wait for him to continue.

"So, Iona saw Eden coming. 'Cause she was the tallest, brightest, best thing to see. Iona started up with the abuse, laughing at her, saying she looked like a fat chicken, not a phoenix. And it was OK at first. Eden just blanked her, kept on. She loved those stilts. She was not gonna let it get to her."

"Iona wouldn't like that," I guessed.

"Too right. You knew her better than me, then. Wish I'd seen it coming."

"What did she do?"

"Iona bloody tripped her, didn't she? She jumped down, ran out, and kicked the stilts. Eden went flying. Face-plant. Right in the road, in front of everyone."

"Yeah, she told me. Lucky she didn't break something."

"She was a bit scraped, not too bad. Think they taught them how to fall, with the stilt training. But when Eden got up, she went for Iona, no holds barred. Proper bitch fight, in the middle of the crowd. Iona's all 'You wouldn't catch me dressing up like some toddler's party' and Eden's like 'You're no part of this. No one wants you here, you don't belong.'

"Iona tries to push her off, telling Eden she's just jealous, but I can see Eden's got to her.

"She keeps at it. Eden tells Iona, 'Stop pretending you don't know. That's the real joke here. You know you don't belong.' I'm trying to pull Eden off Iona, but I've got no idea what she's going on about.

"And Iona's face changes. I can see something is really, badly wrong. Iona tries to hide it, calling Eden a bullshitter, but Eden keeps on at her and that's when Iona goes ballistic.

"She whacks Eden, right in the face. Eden's nose starts bleeding and she's screeching at Iona and they're both covered in blood and everyone's watching and this kid starts crying. It's total chaos. And that's when Eden says it . . ."

"Says what?" I ask slowly, waiting for the bombshell.

"Eden says, 'You're not my blood. See this—it's not the same as yours, is it? You're no sister of mine. You're nothing and you know it.'

"And I think she knows she's gone too far, 'cause she lets me pull her away into the schoolyard, and I get her to sit down and stop the nosebleed, and she's white as a sheet, and there's blood splashed everywhere, over us both."

"So, wait, what was she saying?" I have to get this right. We pause again, in the moonlit woods. Everything seems to have slowed down. The sound of the river fills my head, making it hard to think properly. "That Iona is not her blood? What's that about?" I can't compute the words.

"I dunno. I thought it was their usual drama getting out of hand. Rejecting Iona for being such a bitch, I guess. I just stayed with Eden, tried to calm her down. We went and sat by the river. She was a mess, though. So you see, I couldn't add to it. I couldn't break up with her then, could I?"

I've stopped listening, trying to piece it all together.

Iona is not Eden's blood.

Eden finding three passports back in May. And some papers.

What made Iona change so suddenly?

With a jolt, it clicks into place, the kind of pattern I've been looking for.

I tug at Liam. "Listen. Could it be this: What if Iona was adopted? And Eden wasn't? It happens."

I read a magazine article in one of the endless doctors' waiting rooms, about a couple having IVF, nothing working. Then right after they gave up trying and adopted a kid, the woman fell pregnant naturally. Like being a mum already just flicked the body's switch. What if that happened to Claire?

I tell this to Liam. "What if Iona found out, and that's why she turned against Eden all of a sudden? 'Cause they used to get along, and then it all changed. 'Cause of that bombshell: Iona was adopted; Eden was the birth child."

"It fits with the blood thing . . ."

"It's got to be something that big. Iona wasn't a bitch, not before. But how do you get around something like that? That must be what they argued about, the night Iona died."

"Maybe."

I'm sideswiped by the unfairness of it. "Everyone screws up sometimes. Every family is messed up in its own way: me and Mum, our little two-wheel family. You and your massive busload. You just bump along, doing your best, hoping they know you love them really."

"Yeah, sounds about right." Liam pauses by a stile. He goes first, up three stone steps built into the wall, and then he halts at the top. "We're nearly there. Look!"

Just over the next ridge, higher up the valley, there's a light streaming through the trees, flicking on and off. Liam's silhouette is outlined against the light: red, then blue, then yellow, pulsing in time to a beat we can't hear yet.

"You ready for this bit, Jess? It's gonna be busy. Do you want more time?" he asks.

"We don't have any, remember? Go on, let me through."

The last part is the most dangerous. The path enters the ruins of the old mills. There's a solitary chimney poking up out of the undergrowth. I pick my way across crumbling walls and half-buried slabs of stone.

I have to focus. It's a kind of relief to come back to something so demanding and physical and real. I need to look down, not miss a step, but it doesn't stop the thoughts and images flying around my mind.

If Iona was adopted, would Eden chuck it in her face?

Iona crying, hurting, driving, until—

If it circles my head on a loop, what's it been like for Eden, all summer?

The path gets precarious, about a foot wide, running along the top of a high stone wall.

"You got a flashlight, Jess? Be careful."

"Run this way a hundred times." But I put my phone light on, just to be sure. To our left is a sheer drop, all the way down to the rushing river. To the right are shallow pools, scuzzily dank, covered with lime-green algae and edged with tall weeds. "Shall I go first?" I pretend to be brave, but I remember as a kid needing to be carried along this skinny little ledge of a path. "I always think how weird it is, that people worked here once. Back when this was all modern and new."

"I like it. How quickly the woods grew back. A hundred years ago, this would've been crazy busy. Now look at it."

"Yeah, makes you think, if we stopped now, how quickly we'd be covered over. Like that film, after everyone dies?"

"Yeah, and I bet when they closed the mills, it must've seemed like the end of the world." Liam's with me. He gets it. "And now there's a party in the ruins."

"One day we'll be gone, and some other kids will walk along here." I stop myself. It's all a bit close to home, tonight.

And we're there. I hear the pounding beat echoing off the hillside. I hear distant voices, lots of them, and spots of light like dozens of fireflies in the darkness.

CHAPTER TWENTY-NINE

8:05 p.m.

We reach the clearing in the woods. It's a bowl-shaped space, edged with tall trees, packed with people. The music hasn't ratcheted up yet: It's slow and mellow with a deep bass note I feel in my chest. I see the DJs all set up down there—like this is a theater and that's the stage—with a generator and the projector sending up rainbow lights. People are milling around in groups, sitting in circles, smoking, waiting.

I see Charlotte and Imogen handing out flyers. They haven't given up either, and I feel a surge of affection for them.

"Maybe some of these people don't even know about Eden?" I say, scanning the crowd. I recognize a few faces from school. "So it's our job to tell 'em, find out what they know." I've got my job description and it helps keep the panic at bay. I can do this, it'll be like at work: It's not about me, it's about the task. I try to break the crowd down into manageable chunks. I can deal with two or three people at a time.

I leave Liam and grab at Imo and Charlotte as they get near. "Hi. How's it going? Can I see your flyer?"

"Hey, Jess." Charlotte greets me in a hoarse whisper, as though she's been crying too. "What a nightmare. Did you see it on the news?"

I shake my head. "Been out looking all day. Nothing. Did the police come to your place too? What did they say?"

"Not a lot. Questions mainly." Charlotte sounds beyond tired. All her perkiness is long gone. "They said they're exploring all the lines of inquiry, whatever that means."

"It's getting late, isn't it?" Imo looks different. This morning was an act, but it's sunk in now. She's shaky. Her mask isn't there. "Do you really think she's all right?" She clutches at my arm like a drowning person. I'm sure it's the first time she's ever touched me, and I don't even mind. "Jess, tell me the truth?"

"My mum told me about her text. Saying good-bye. It doesn't have to be that. What if she met someone?"

"Who?"

In answer, I look through the crowds and my gaze falls on someone I recognize: Tyler. He's with some of his mates from last weekend. I need to talk to him.

"I don't know. We're just guessing, that's all. Can I see the flyer?"

She gives me one and I hold it up, shining my phone flashlight on it. It's the same stuff we put on social media, only somehow it feels more real, holding it in my hand. Eden's face in black and white, smiling, beautiful. Fair hair, white teeth. It makes it seem as though she belongs in the past already.

Was Iona really not her sister? Have I guessed right? I always thought they looked alike. But maybe I just saw what I expected.

"Can I have some?" I ask. "I'll help."

"Thanks, Jess." Charlotte passes me a sheaf of flyers, with a quick, grateful smile.

"Take care," Imo says.

Their politeness is chilling. I hate that it's taken today to make them accept me.

I turn away and start working my way around the edge of the crowd, keeping my eyes on Tyler as I circle toward him. "Tyler! Hey."

"Jess," he says. I'm surprised he remembers my name. "Any news?" He taps me gently on the arm in greeting.

I take a step back, reading him, recalling that he's number two on my list of suspects. "Not yet, but my mum said they're starting search parties in town."

"Yeah, I'm heading down to join in. Just came here in case she was . . ."

Really? Same plan as me. Or is that what the guilty man says to blend in? I'm too exhausted to act like the police, asking the right question and working out what he means by the answer. "Did you speak to Eden, after last Saturday?"

"Sure." Now he looks surprised. "Didn't she say? We met up Tuesday night. Late. We were gonna meet last night too, but she didn't reply. . . ."

"Last night?" If he was guilty, surely he wouldn't admit that? Blink once: He's a stranger, setting up secret late-night meetings with Eden. Blink twice: He's kind and concerned, going out of his way for a girl he just met.

"Thought she told you everything?" Tyler is saying. "She said you two were tight."

Ridiculously, I feel betrayed. What else did she tell Tyler about me? "We are." I try not to sound defensive. Or we were. I feel, with every new fact I learn, Eden's getting farther away from me. She's on the deck of a ship, heading out to sea, leaving me stranded.

"She'll be a'right, Jess. It's no one's fault," Tyler tells me gently, leaning in. "She's coming outta rough times: her sister's accident, just after the adoption papers an' all that . . ."

My jaw actually drops. I didn't realize that was a real thing till now, when my mouth is hanging open. "She told you that?" I'm not going to admit she only told me half of it and I had to guess the rest.

"Yeah, last Saturday. We didn't get much sleep—" He sees my face. "Nah, not like that. Well, not *just* like that. I mean, we talked. Really talked. You might say we clicked."

That triggers such a stupid mixture of jealousy and relief that I almost laugh out loud, but there's something in his eyes that stops me. His big brown eyes are serious and concerned. I think he's telling me the truth.

"OK, good. I'm glad you clicked, really." And I am glad, at the back of my mind, below all the worry, 'cause me and Liam clicked too, and maybe, just maybe, there's a way out of this, if we find Eden safe and well. That *if* is fragile, crumbling minute by minute.

"She's battled some demons, but she's gonna come through, ain't she, Jess?"

I can't say: *I know Eden best, and even my faith is fading.* I don't want to take away his hope. Instead, I take his number and hug him awkwardly around my bundle of flyers. I realize dimly that I've touched more people today than in the last ten months put together, and with everything else that's going on, it's been the least of my worries. "We'll keep looking for her. We won't give up. See you at the search party, yeah?"

But as soon as I leave Tyler, I start spiraling fast again. I'm not helped by the bittersweet music and the sight of two girls from school crying over a crumpled flyer, Eden's face all twisted sideways on it. Then I have a horrible thought.

If Eden died, would we be the chief mourners? Me, Liam, Imogen, Charlotte, now Tyler too. We are Eden's best friends. Would we be near the front at her funeral? Would we stand and speak about what she meant to us? Would I write a poem that made people cry?

I try to imagine a world without Eden in it, but it is impossible. It's like imagining no more sun.

The pain in my chest feels like a bomb about to explode. Is this it? Is this what I'm facing? Life without Eden.

Tick, tick, tick . . .

I can't go on. It hurts too much. I do not want to go forward into that future without her. I fold my arms across my chest to contain the ticking bomb, as if I can squash it down and stop it from destroying me.

That's when it happens.

My phone buzzes and I pull it out, expecting Mum again.

It's Eden.

Her mobile. Not her landline.

Eden.

CHAPTER THIRTY

8:35 p.m.

Eden! My fingers are stupid, swollen, clumsy. I nearly drop the phone. I nearly hit REJECT in my panic.

"Eden? Eden, is that you?"

I can't hear anything.

"Eden? Eden?" I sink down on the slope, the flyers drifting around my feet like snow. I jam one hand over my ear to block out the music. "Where are you? What happened? Are you there? *Eden?*"

Silence.

"Are you OK? Eden, are you OK?" I hardly know what I'm saying. I still can't hear her. A plane burrs overhead. I hear that in stereo, with the slow bass.

Icy fingers squeeze my heart. What if she's hurt? What if she's trying to speak but she can't? She might've fallen. She might've broken something.

"Eden? Eden, tell me you're OK!"

I think I can hear someone breathing. Listening.

"Eden?"

I press the phone harder to my ear, but I can still only hear the bloody plane and the music, distantly.

What if she's hurt herself and she didn't want to be alone as she slipped away?

"Eden, if you can hear me, hang on, OK? Just tell me where you are? Everything's going to be OK. Just let me help, please?"

Silence. A deeper silence this time. I can't hear the breathing now, or the plane, or the music.

"*Eden!*" I scream it.

A horrible thought slithers in and coils around my brain. What if it's not Eden? What if someone's got her?

"OK, you listen to me." I try to sound brave, but it's one of the hardest things I've ever had to do. The phone wobbles against the side of my face because my fingers are trembling so hard. "If you can hear me . . . if that's someone else, just stay calm. Tell me where you are—"

The line goes dead. Whoever phoned me has hung up.

"No, no, no. You can't. No!"

I call her back. Straight to voice mail. Redial, redial.

I sit there in shock. My mind is a jumble, a deck of cards chucked to the ground. Which ones do I pick up first? I have to tell Liam.

First I ring Mum.

"Mum? It's me. No, don't lecture. Stop! Listen to me!" Words pour out of me, a torrent that is so strong she can't swim against it. "Eden just rang me, or her phone did. I couldn't hear anything. Nothing! Just now. But she hung up, and now she's not answering. You've got to ring Claire." I find the strength to give orders. "Tell the police. Quick. I have to go. In case she rings again. Now, Mum, please!"

I hang up, gripping my phone tightly in my hand, as if it's the most precious thing in the world.

My legs feel like chewed grass. I get up and stagger down the hill.

Tick, tick, tick . . .

The clock's speeded up. Countdown.

Come on, Jess, think! What's really happening here? What would Eden do? What tipped her over the edge? Eden lost her sister. Her only sister, whatever their history.

Then it hits me. Now I know the whole story, I know where Eden is. I know where she'd go.

CHAPTER THIRTY-ONE

8:38 p.m.

I break into a run, looking for Liam. I can't do this alone. I need him. If Eden's not alone, or if she's hurt, it's going to take more than me. . . . I push through bodies, uncaring.

The music sounds louder now, and I realize I'm right: She *is* near here. When we were talking, I heard the bass of the music and the plane passing overhead at the same time—over the phone *and* right here. The plane noise might carry for miles, but not the music. It has to be nearby. I must be right.

Tick, tick, tick . . .

This is the end of the race. Adrenaline gives me wings. I push on, shouting, "Liam? Where's Liam Caffrey?"

People stare at me, faces blank as masks, split in two, light and shade.

I blunder through. "Liam?" My voice gets high and desperate. I need him more than I want to admit. "Liam!"

Suddenly, there is space. There is Liam. And there is Josh Clarkson. My heart sinks.

In front of the DJ deck, flanked by two huge speakers, there's a gap where there should be dancing. People nervously cluster in a circle around Liam and Josh.

"Liam!" I shout. "Liam! She rang me! Eden's phone rang me!" But he's not listening. Josh is right in his face.

"Come on, shithead, what did you do to her?" Josh is taunting Liam, loud and slurring.

"Get lost, Clarkson, I didn't touch her. I wouldn't."

Josh is shoving Liam in the chest and circling him. Unsteady, on his toes, like he thinks they're in *Fight Club* or something.

The stupid colored lights give us all a front-row view of the circus.

Josh's still holding a can in his left hand, slopping beer as he jabs with his right fist. His boy-band hair flops in lank strips, and his pretty-boy face is as screwed up as a snarling dog's.

"Liam! Stop it. Listen—I need to tell you something!" My voice sounds weak and strangled. I try to get closer, but my body has other ideas. There is no way it's going near a fight. My legs are shaking so much I can't trust them right now. This is ridiculous. It's like I'm stuck on an old setting. I need to override it. I will do it, for Eden's sake.

"That's not what I heard, you fucker." *Jab.* Josh's too drunk to hide his jealousy. He throws his can behind him.

"So?" Liam's jaw juts tight. "She's not your property. She gets to choose who she's with."

"Liam!" I try again, but he can't hear me with Josh blocking him. I can't move. I look around me for help, scanning the faces, illuminated green, blue, and yellow.

Tyler is there. He meets my eyes, sees the state I'm in. He starts pushing through the crowd. But before he can speak—

"She was *my* girlfriend first. Bastard!" Josh screams, and launches himself at Liam. He grabs him by his T-shirt and slams him up against the speaker behind them. He pulls his arm back and throws a punch. Liam ducks and the force of the blow topples the speaker backward, taking both of them with it.

The music cuts out.

The speaker hits the ground and they roll off, tumbling onto the ground. People scatter, getting out of their way, but then coming back in for a better view, like all this is a spectator sport.

I'm trying to get a grip, my hands on my thighs, gulping down air. I can't help it. I sink slowly, letting people surge forward past me to see. *Come on, Jess, this isn't aimed at you.* I manage to stand. I take a wobbling step toward them. I can do this. For Eden's sake. I can. I take control. I go closer.

I see Josh yelling in Liam's face, slamming his fist down again and again. Liam twists aside. He jumps to his feet, furious now. Even in this light, I can see his cheek swelling red around a white blaze. His hair's all tufted up.

They face off, like two fighting dogs. Circling. Liam's ready, fists up, defensive. He's taller and stronger than Josh. And sober.

"Yeah? Think you're hard enough? Think again, Caffrey," Josh screeches. "I know about you. What you're like. Scum."

Everyone looks at Liam. He doesn't answer. I see the tension in his jaw.

"Go on, wanna hit me again?" Josh yells. "I can take it. It'll be worth it to see the back of you. Second offense, with your record? They'll throw away the fucking keys. Do it! Fucking do it!"

I throw myself forward, past Tyler, into the ring, into the fight, for Eden. "Liam! Don't. Stop. Come with me!"

He hears me now all right. Everyone hears me in the shocking silence.

"Come on; Eden rang me. She needs us. *Now!*"

Tyler spins, as if he's magnetized by the news. I don't care about him. I stare at Liam. He has to listen, after all it cost me to reach him.

Liam looks back at me, and I think he's with me. I think he's going to follow me.

Josh spits in Liam's face.

That's when Liam cracks. I see him grab Josh's shirt and pull him up, his fist raised.

I give up. I turn on my heel. I'll do this alone if I have to.

CHAPTER THIRTY-TWO

9:06 p.m.

I ring Eden's phone, leave a message on her voice mail. "I'm coming, E. Wait for me, please. I'm on my way. Hang in there." I flee from the clearing, stumbling and clutching at tree trunks. My mouth tastes sour and dry with fear.

I take the quickest route—up the hill to the old pack-horse trail just above the tree line, where massive stones are set into the ground—a centuries-old highway. My feet skim over the smooth weathered stones, like whalebacks surfacing from the close-grazed grass.

I speed up. I'm almost running on empty, but as at the end of a race, my body finds more. It changes gear, surprising me.

Eden wanted what she couldn't have: to make it right with her sister. That's impossible, so what's the next best thing? The place they'd been happiest. I'm sure Eden went there. That's where she is right now. That's where I'm going.

I'm trusting what I know about Eden. I'm trusting all our years together.

If I'm wrong, I'm out of ideas, out of luck, out of time.

I'm going to the place Iona loved, up this valley, near their old house—the one from the old photo in their hallway, where they'd been happy. I'm going to the river, Iona's favorite spot, only two fields down from their old house. I'm going to that place, to the circle carved into the valley like a cupped palm, so the sun gets trapped there, where the river flows into a sweet round pool, just deep enough to swim. I'm going to that place, where we spent hours exploring upstream, making dams, clambering over rocks, skimming stones, throwing sticks for the farmer's crazy collie. I'm going there, where Iona took us for long summer afternoons, where we'd eat bilberries till our mouths were stained purple, where we stayed all day till we were sunburned and soaked through.

It was heaven for Iona.

It's everything Eden's lost.

It's where she would go to feel close to her sister.

Or to join her.

I hurry over the last large stones, vault the stile, and I'm almost there, descending to that place, ducking down to the river. The moon is enough now. The pale gray path shines in the moonlight. A ghost path, beckoning me on.

"Let her be there. Please. Let her be alive!" I whisper to the rhythm of my rushing feet. I pray to the moon, to the woods, to the pale horizon.

It must be a shadow, a cloud over the moon, like a blinking

eye. The light changes. I swear the world is listening. The night air is alive around me.

"I'll do anything! Let her be alive."

The world waits. *It's not enough.*

What can I give?

"Let me be in time. If she's alive, I'll give up Liam."

It's what I want most, next to this, so it has to be that. I feel my sacrifice ripping out of me, painful and real.

"I'll do it, I promise. I'll do the right thing; I'll give him up. Just let Eden be alive!"

My prayer ripples out into the night. I picture it: a little flimsy, feathered wish. It flies up, changing the fabric of space and time. I can't bring back the dead, but I can restore this balance. I can give up my first love, for her.

My feet change rhythm as I hit the descent: staccato, off-beat steps. I see the river through the trees.

I need to be careful. I slow down. I silence my feet.

I pick my way over the last stones, and then dart over the little packhorse bridge: nothing more than two vast stones laid right across the river. I hide in the shadow of a slender tree, searching the wide moonlit palm of the valley.

Finish line? Or failure?

I stand there, every nerve strung tight, ready to run or fight or scream for help. I leave the bridge and tiptoe across the grass, scanning left to right, left to right. My eyes strain into the darkness. I see nothing moving in the dark blue shadows. There's no one here. I'm wrong. I've failed.

I swing round, ready to howl at the moon.

That's when I see her.

Eden's there. Lying on the big rock. Her hair streams out, white gold in the moonlight, like she's a fairy-tale princess. One hand hangs limply down.

I fall on my knees.

CHAPTER THIRTY-THREE

9:32 p.m.

I am a ghost. I'm pale and papery. I have no substance. I have no idea how I cross the space between us.

I'm too late. Do I touch her? I dare not.

Somehow, I climb up.

If there's someone else here, I've stopped caring. I've found Eden. Nothing else matters.

Her skin is ivory and perfect. Her eyes are closed.

I can't even tell if she's breathing.

I can't tell if I am.

Something crinkles under my elbow. It's a foil packet of pills. No bigger than my hand, and yet it's done this? I hold it up to the shaking light of my phone, reading the weird brand name, trying to see how many of the small white ovals have been pushed through the layer of foil. I count, trembling, and find six little empty nests of crumpled plastic. Six? Is that enough to die?

"Don't leave me. No!"

I can't believe I've come all this way, too late.

I can't believe she's dead.

"Eden, Eden, no . . ." My tears drip onto her face.

My tears.

Not a kiss.

This is what wakes her.

"Jess. You came."

Her skin is warm. Her hair is warm. She is real and alive and warm.

I collapse onto the rock next to her. I hug her to me, so tightly I can even feel her heart, pounding out the truth.

The bomb inside me melts instead of exploding. I'm a river. I'm a flood. I'm crying and gasping. This must be hysteria, but happy. I stutter and sob. I'm tears and snot. I'm pure gratitude. I will never, ever complain of anything again.

Eden is alive.

"Of course I came. I'm so glad you rang." I sniff and rub at my face. "But why didn't you say something? What if I'd guessed wrong?"

She doesn't answer me. And then I realize: What about the pills?

It occurs to me in a horrible rush, this might be false relief. She's alive now, sure, but what has she done? "Is that why you didn't speak? 'Cause you didn't want me to find you? Have you taken these?" I fumble on the rock, up on my elbows. "Tell me. Eden, what have you done?" I realize I can smell whiskey; that's the stale whiff on her hoodie. I shake the packet of pills in her face. "What is this stuff? How many have you had? When did you take them?"

"I haven't. All right? I was going to, last night, but I haven't . . ." Eden sounds strange. Her words are slurring, her eyes won't focus on me.

"So why are they here?" She must've taken them. She's taken them and she's lying to me, so the pills have time to work. "Some are gone. Oh my God, Eden . . . what did you do?"

"I was gonna chuck them away, OK?" She doesn't sound like herself. She's trembling. She's ashen and shaking, mumbling at me. "They're Mum's. She's got 'em from the doctor, after Iona . . . I wasn't going to take them. Well, I was, but . . ."

"What do you mean, you were going to take them?"

"I didn't know what to do. . . . I wanted to tell you, talk to you."

"Have you taken any?"

"No. I changed my mind. But I didn't know how to come home. . . ." She's whispering so low I can hardly hear her.

Now I'm really scared.

I ring 999 because I can't trust her to tell me the truth about this, not if she's already decided to die. I hold on to her tightly with my free hand, gripping her hoodie as if she's a hyperactive toddler, so she can't run off again, even though I can feel all the fight has gone out of her.

"What service do you need?" a man's voice asks me.

"*What service?* Oh, an ambulance! Quick. And the police will need to know. . . ." I give our location, Eden's name. Tell him she's the missing girl, alive, but I don't know what she's taken. I spell out the brand name of the pills, feeling like I've just called her a liar.

Afterward, Eden doesn't speak. It seems very quiet, and we just sit there, hunched up next to each other, with the river gurgling away like it always does, even if your world is ending. I take my hoodie out of my backpack and try to cover her with it.

Tugging the fabric around Eden creates a layer of normality, as if we're just having a sleepover or something, trying to get comfy as we talk all night. But she might be dying, and this might be our last chance to say it all. In the moonlight, our world's gone eerie and surreal.

"I'm sorry, E." I wrap my arm around her shoulder and try to pull her close to me, for warmth. "I know about Iona. What you were going to tell me, about her being adopted. But you can't blame yourself for what happened. And it's no reason to do *this*!"

"How do you know that, Jess?" She pulls away, still slurring.

I can see her eyes, heavy-lidded, struggling to stay open. A new spiral of pain starts mining down into my heart. "No, Eden. Don't you fall asleep. Stay with me!" I slap her cheek gently.

"Get off me. Anyway, what do you know about my reasons?" She's back, glaring at me from under her lashes. "S'my turn to be the grieving fuckup. You had your go!"

"Well, you don't get to give up! I didn't give up, did I?"

"It's my turn. My rules. And I choose when it's game over. . . ."

"Oh, we're playing a game now? What's that, then: Top Trumps of Pain?" I'm actually angry with her, even if she is dying. "Yeah, OK, you win. Death of a sister beats old-news hate crime hands down!"

She has her eyes closed, curling into a ball.

I shake her arm, trying to wake her up. "Is that what you were playing at today?" I ask her, my voice cracking into tears. "Going for the prize in the game of *I hurt so much I'm going to kill myself*? '*Look, I'm dead, so I win!*' And the great thing is how much you fuck up the rest of us who are left behind, so we never forgive ourselves for the rest of our lives. And we don't even get to answer back."

I don't know who's talking. I don't sound like me. I sound stronger than I feel. Have I changed so much today? "I was there for you this summer. Just like you were there for me before. It's what we do. I bloody love you. I'm glad you're alive. Thinking you were dead today, it nearly killed me."

I can't tell if she's listening. She's leaning forward now, all tense and trembly, with her hair hanging in her face, so I can't see her expression.

"The thing is, if you kill yourself, Eden Holby, you know what? You take me with you. What's my life without you in it? So you just think about that."

"I did think about that. You and Liam, you'd be fine. I know you like him. I know what happened at the party." She turns her head slowly to face me, all pale in the milky darkness, her eyes like huge dark pools. "Was I not hurting enough?"

Her words cut me.

"I'm sorry," I whisper, all my fight gone. "It just ha—"

"Don't you dare tell me it just happened. Bullshit. S'always a choice. I knew he'd choose you in the end. *Little Jess*. Little bird with a broken wing . . ."

Her knife goes deeper.

I take a breath. "OK, yeah, I screwed up. I fell in love with Liam. If it makes it any better, it happened years ago, but I never said. I never did anything! I buried it, OK? It was just that night. He was so sad when you went off with Tyler—"

"So it's my fault? As usual."

"No. Listen to me for once. You don't listen enough." You'd think that I'd be more gentle, if she'd taken pills and was slipping away, but suddenly the most important thing is to be honest. Even if we've only got a bit of time. Especially then. I think she likes it too. She almost smiles, a little flicker, and shuts up for once.

"Yes, I love Liam, but I love you more," I tell her. "Liam knows that. He loves you too. We've been looking bloody everywhere for you, E. We've walked miles." I slump forward, and I'm shattered suddenly. I'm completely done in. I've got nothing left. I want to go to sleep, leaning against her.

"I love you too. Honest. I just got stuck." She sounds stronger now, more normal. Maybe she's just tired and hungover, not overdosed after all? She's been missing from home a night and a day. When did she eat or sleep? No wonder she can't stay awake. Maybe she's telling the truth.

A spark, then a little flicker of hope, starts burning inside me. I feel her arm work its way around my shoulders.

We hug, properly, at last. Like hundreds of times before. Like never before. I can feel her skin, her shoulder blades beneath my fingertips, and even after everything, her hair smells so right, all fresh and appley and just like her.

We cling to each other.

"Where did you go, Eden?" I can't help myself; I just blurt it out, into her hair.

She takes a deep ragged breath. "Liam walked me home, after we had a fight. Split up, finally."

What? He never mentioned it.

"And yes, I know, what did I expect, after Saturday?"

I don't react. I just listen.

"I was gonna have a drink, then sneak out to meet Tyler. Did that Tuesday night. Said I'd meet him again. But I couldn't. Was like hitting a wall. I was tired of hurting. Tired of being sad and guilty. I wanted to sleep, forever. So I got Mum's pills, a bottle of Dad's whiskey. I went out and I just walked."

Her walking boots had been missing—that was what I'd almost noticed at her house. So I had been right about the sandals.

"I walked and walked, all night. I got near Stoodley Pike just before morning. It seemed like the right place. Lonely, but I knew there'd be walkers next day, to find . . . me. I texted Mum, to say sorry."

Shit. I bite down my words. I won't interrupt.

"I was going to do it. These pills, washed down with whiskey. I drank a bit first, for courage. I thought I'd just go to sleep. Seemed an OK way to go. But I spilled the bloody whiskey all down me, hands were shaking with cold and whatever . . . I've never been good at swallowing pills with no drink."

She sounds more normal now, dreamy, as if she's telling me a bedtime story.

"It got light. The clouds were lovely, Jess, all pale and pearly. It did look a bit like heaven. Got me thinking about Iona. How much she'd want to live, if she could. If she had the choice, she wouldn't die. She had so much she wanted to do.

"So I couldn't do it. I couldn't chuck it all away, in case it did get better in the end. I thought of Mum and Dad finding me. I thought of you. I couldn't do it, Jess, I couldn't."

She crumples now, her lovely face all blotchy and sobbing and snotty.

I sit quietly, being patient. Being her rock. When she calms a bit, I offer her the sleeve of the hoodie and she wipes her cheeks on it. "So what did you do?"

"I lay there, freezing cold. Then I went up the tower and sat there, watching it get properly light. When the sun came up, I could see all the hills and woods and farms and houses, right across the valley. It was so beautiful, Jess. . . ." She fades out for a bit. Then tries again. "Was like I'd been given a chance. A new day. I needed to think. I didn't want to walk back into the same crap. . . ."

"Where were you? I looked all over. . . ."

"Just walking. Across the top of the moor. Walking. Thinking. Trying to answer all my questions. Then I went to our old house. I saw the new people. Little kids coming in from school: two girls on our trampoline. Like me 'n' Iona. Like we used to be." She cries harder for a bit. "Me and Iona, before—we were happy, weren't we?"

I squeeze her arm. "Yeah, you really were." Eden and Iona, running wild in the fields, walking to the village school, still friends. It was when the family moved that everything changed.

"I'm not kidding myself? I mean, those bits are just as real, right?" She gulps her sobs down. "Now Iona is dead, you can see her whole life. And it's OK to remember further back . . . the good bits."

"Course it is, E," I tell her. "I've been doing that. Bet everyone has."

"Anyway, it's what I've been thinking about today. And I wanted more. I wanted to go back to the best bits, you know? So I came here."

I nod. I do know.

"But she isn't here. She's not coming back. I have to face it. That this is the hardest thing ever. That I miss her. That I love her. And she didn't know." She fades out and I feel her take a huge breath.

"Jess, I need you to know what I did, that night. The night she died . . ."

"It's OK." I can hear how much this is hurting her. "You don't have to say it. . . ."

"J, let me tell you the worst. And you can judge me, or whatever. But I need to get it out, OK?"

"OK," I tell her, hugging her a little tighter.

"After we fought at the parade, it was cold war. She knew I knew, the adoption stuff, but we didn't talk about it. I was so angry. Fighting back."

"Well, you'd taken it long enough . . . ," I say gently, but she shushes me. I know she just needs to speak.

"Kicked off at dinner. She was smirking at me, till I snapped at her. Dad lost it, said all he wanted was for us to eat a meal like a normal family.

"So I said we weren't. We'd never be a normal family. Dad started yelling at me to apologize. Anyway, I blew up. Told them they were all liars."

I wince. "Shit."

"Hitting fan. Yeah. Iona didn't realize. She laughed at me, all *look who's in trouble now*, for a change. She always knew how to push my buttons. I flipped. Picked up my glass and threw it at her. It shattered on the wall, bits flying everywhere. Iona's arm started bleeding. Dad went mental. Told me to get out."

I can feel her getting more rigid and tense in my arms.

"So I said Iona should get out, not me, seeing as she was the one who didn't belong. I didn't mean it. I just wanted to hurt her back, like she'd been hurting me. Jess, I called her a stray dog. Asked if they got her down at the rescue center."

It's like she's reading out lines, as a punishment, but she keeps on, grimly.

"I said it was no wonder she was such a bitch; her real mum was probably some psycho junkie whore. That's when Mum slapped me."

"Your mum?" I'm shocked.

"Yeah, first time for everything. She's never hit either of us. Never."

"What did you do?"

"Ran upstairs. Heard Iona slam the front door and drive off in Mum's car. Mum and Dad, they'd had a few Friday-night drinks, so they couldn't go after her. I tried to say sorry. Dad said I'd done enough damage for one night.

"Waiting was grim. I think I fell asleep on the sofa for a bit. It was just light when the police came. . . . Mum screaming. Dad crying. I'd never seen my dad cry before."

I can't speak. My eyes are full of tears as I hold her.

"I'm so sorry for today." She's breaking down now too. I feel her sobs, her ribs shaking. "It just hurt so much, I couldn't keep on going. I'm not that strong. I can't . . ."

She pulls back, and I see her mouth fall open in a wide O of pure pain, and for once, Eden Holby is as ugly as the grief that shakes her.

"Yes, you can. And you will. And we'll be there with you." I don't let her go. I hold on as she howls it out and I cry right along with her, longer than I think possible, till finally we're done.

We're damp and wrung out, shipwrecked on that stupid rock.

"It seemed like the only thing left for me to do. Iona's dead and it's my fault and I can't make it right. I can't bring her back and I can't say sorry. My parents are destroyed and I can't fix it. I can only show how bad I feel, how sorry I am."

"What, by taking away the only thing they have left?" I can't believe she could be so stupid.

"Yeah, OK, so I got there in the end. That's why I'm still here. And 'cause of you. An' Tyler. And him."

When I lift my head from her shoulder, there's someone in a pale blue T-shirt coming along the far bank, faster, faster, faster. . . .

Liam is too impatient to go around and cross the bridge. He splashes through the water at the top of the weir. "Eden? Eden! Is that you?" he shouts in a voice that I've not heard before.

And she slides off, scraping and bumping her way down. She goes to him.

Eden and Liam stand in the river, embracing so tightly they're one figure. A tall shape, lit from behind with the projections still beaming into the sky from the party down the valley. Together they're a lighthouse. So no one is ruined on the rocks.

I get up, shivering now too, and slip down to the grassy bank, only skinning one of my palms on the way.

The wail of a siren floats down from the village road. In the opposite direction to the party, I see the lights of the search-and-rescue team coming down the bridleway toward us, their headlamps flashing in and out of the trees. I hear their dogs barking and men's voices.

I don't say anything. I leave Liam and Eden together. I walk back over the bridge and I flee.

CHAPTER THIRTY-FOUR

10:20 p.m.

I use the flashlight on my phone to light my way and I stumble down the valley back to the party. I follow the music to the clearing. When I get there, Imogen and Charlotte home straight in on me, starving for news.

"Eden's alive," I tell them. "Rescue team have her. Up there."

We actually hug. Me, Imogen, Charlotte. So I'm no longer the smelly goth? I'm not on the outside anymore. I'm one of them. We're all in it, all of us. All so different, but all here right now. I look over their shoulders at the moonlit clearing.

"*Who-who?*" the owl asks, sounding like it belongs in the music.

I wonder what the owls think of all this. They don't stress about difference, do they? You don't find an owl being jealous of a deer 'cause it can't run; it knows it has wings.

Am I crazy? These feel like mad thoughts. I think I might be totally unhinged now. My mind's seen too much, been too far today.

"It's going to be OK," Imogen tells me.

"Everything!" Charlotte agrees. She's still holding flyers. She throws them up into the air, laughing, and the papers twist down, catching the rainbow lights.

I can't speak, but I smile and I nod and then I turn away from Imo and Charlotte and wade deep into the crowd. I nearly laugh out loud, 'cause I actually feel safe here, deep in the middle of dancing bodies. It's not about me: Each person is lost in the music, and I dive in too. The rhythm grounds me. I can hold on to that. It tethers my body, and my mind can float off with the melody, with the woman's voice, so pure and fierce, and I follow the piano that comes in next, taking me somewhere high and free, like a spiral up to the stars. For the first time in a very long time, I let go completely.

The wind kicks up, sending clouds sailing across the sky. The moon goes in and out again, hiding between the clouds, tinting the world silver and black, black and then silver, like an old film flickering. There are strobe lights in the DJ deck, and the moon joins in, scattering cutouts on the ground, stark and crisp, appearing and disappearing. I see my body, my shadow, black on white, hair flying loose, arms out. Is that me? I look free.

I dance, and as I move I know that I'm whole again. I will survive. I did survive. They didn't destroy me, though they came close.

I made it through, with the help of Mum, Eden. And, yes, Liam.

Eden made it too.

I know she's going to be OK. She's at the start of a path. The start of life without Iona. This summer was the crisis, the shock of it. All anger and denial. Now she can start to mourn.

I dance on. And I start to mourn too. With wet cheeks, I dance for Iona. I finally admit to my sadness, my little grief that was so insignificant next to Eden's that I couldn't pay it any attention. But my heart is breaking for the Iona we lost, for the one-off girl she was, an almost-big-sister to me, before she got shunted onto the wrong track, before she had a chance to make it right.

I dance and I cry for the future she won't have, for the forgiveness she never knew, for her friends and all the ones out there who were waiting for her, whom she'll never meet now.

I dance for Eden and the big black hole in her heart.

I'm so light now, I feel I could break loose and float up over the valley. I'd see it from above, like the owl. Did Iona see this, as she left us? The steep craggy slopes where they hewed out stone and built this town. The houses, all snug and close, huddling in the valley bottom, looped by the curving lines of the canal, the railway, the river, and the road, all holding our town in their arms. The old chimneys, the ruins and the new-builds, all that life going on, right here. And we will be part of it: me, Eden, Liam.

Liam. I dance for him too. Thinking of him now is like pressing a bruise. I dance and I say good-bye to him. I dance myself farther away from him, but this time it doesn't work.

Instead, I conjure him up. I open my eyes at last and I see him, coming through the shadowy dancing bodies, his T-shirt catching flashes of light: blue, green, yellow.

It's really him. Standing right in front of me. Filling my vision.

CHAPTER THIRTY-FIVE

11:30 p.m.

"Jess!"

"What's wrong? Where is she?" I can't see his face well enough to read it. "What happened?" I can't think why he would leave her.

"It's OK. Everything's OK." Liam has to shout over the music. "Come over here so we can talk?"

We edge through the press of bodies and find a quieter corner, behind two huge trees. My legs buckle and I slide down, leaning against the bark, knees pulled up. I rest my head on my leggings, feeling like I've been wearing these clothes for at least a hundred years. "Tell me," I whisper.

"Jess, you should've seen it." He slides down at my side. "The search-and-rescue team came down, with dogs and stretchers and stuff. They checked Eden over, wrapped her in blankets, gave her energy drinks. They got her up to the pub's parking lot and that's when her folks came. And the police, ambulance, the lot. Swarming around her." His voice breaks. "Her mum and her dad—it was . . . she was . . . kind of *squashed* between them. They were sobbing, losing it." He takes a breath and lets it out slowly. "Intense. After a bit, her dad tried to thank me. 'Cept he couldn't really speak. I told him it wasn't me, it was you he should thank. Dunno if it went in. Don't think anything went in, 'cept Eden being safe. She's really safe, Jess. You did it. You found her."

"Yeah." I can't think what else to say. Part of me is still flying over the valley, weightless. "Why didn't you stay? Where's she gone?"

"Home. Her mum wasn't taking any shit. The medics did some checks right there, but Claire said the rest could wait; they were going home."

"Good." I'm glad for Claire and Simon.

"Jess, she sent me to find you—Eden did." He turns sideways so I can see his expression. "We grabbed a second while Claire was arguing with the uniforms."

"What do you mean? Is she all right? What did she say?" I'm not taking any chances here.

"Eden told me to find you, Jess. To be with you." He smiles properly, and it's like a camera flash; I can't see anything but the afterburn. "That you needed me. So here I am."

A warm glow starts firing up inside me. I hug myself, keeping it in, keeping my eyes on his, not daring to believe him. "Are you sure?"

Liam nods. "Not the kind of thing I get wrong." He nudges me. "What do you say?"

"I can't. Not now." I look down. If I don't meet his gaze, I'm brave enough to tell him. "When I was looking for her, I made a deal." It sounds crazy now, so I drop my voice to a whisper. "I promised I'd give you up if Eden was OK. And she is, so we can't . . . I can't. I gave you up for Eden."

"Well, she doesn't want me." He laughs and breaks off when I still don't look up. "It's finished, but we're both OK with that." He sits up. "Oi, anyway, why is it up to you? Or even her? What about me? What about what I want? Look at me, Jess!"

I sneak a quick glance. His eyebrows are telling me something urgent.

"And a deal with *who*? Jess, it doesn't work like that."

"Who says?" I want to believe him. I want to touch him. I want to kiss his neck. I want to be closer, breathing him in. But it's not right. I promised. I remember the pale moonlit path of stones, how I felt the world listening. Could I have heard it wrong?

Liam swears. "Don't you get it, Jess? Even after everything. Why is it OK for random bad things to happen, but you can't let random good things happen? You don't owe anybody for what happened today. You don't have to give up what you want. If Eden says this is OK, who else can stop us?" And then, like the wind changing, I see the doubts blow in. Anxious, he runs a hand through his hair, tufting it higher. "Unless you don't want this. *Jess?* Is this your way of telling me to get lost and leave you alone?"

"No." I reach out and take his hand. Its weight and warmth are familiar now. My hand fits in his. "It's not that. Just, what about Eden? It's too soon. We've got to put her first."

"And you can. Go see her tomorrow if you don't believe me. I don't mind waiting. Listen, I wasn't telling you everything, before. 'Cause I didn't know how you felt. This morning you said we should forget about Saturday. . . ."

"What do you mean?"

"I met up with Eden last night to be honest with her, to finish it. Only it got messy. Think we both felt guilty 'bout Saturday . . ." He breathes out in a rush. "Anyway, I was right. She does want Tyler. She told me yesterday. And I saw him just now, on the phone to her."

It fits with what Tyler said. I look past Liam, at the magical silvery woods. I feel hope rising like water springing up from the earth, gathering speed as it rushes downstream. Is Liam right? Can I have it all? Me and Liam and Eden too? All of us together and no one lost? It's been so hard this year, I can't believe I'm allowed something easy, something good.

"And another thing. I didn't do it. I didn't hit Josh this time. I wanted to." He swears. "God, I wanted to. But I just pushed him off and ran after you—only I guessed the wrong path first time, so it took me longer to find you."

"I'm glad you didn't. He isn't worth it." But I still haven't said yes, and he knows it.

Liam shakes his hand free, digging out a cigarette and lighting it, still talking restlessly. "None of it is fixed. It's not *fate*. What do you think, Jess?" He waves the lit end of his cigarette around as he gestures wildly. "You think there's someone watching us, with a giant pair of scales, weighing what we're owed? Anyway, if there was, I think you've suffered enough, don't you? We don't get to be happy or unhappy 'cause we deserve it. Do you think Iona deserved to die?"

"Course not." I shake my head, trying to follow his logic, like a safety line hauling me up.

"We're just lucky if we get good stuff. But you still have to choose what to make of it, right? So let's grab it, Jess, why not? I'm up for it, if you are."

I sit up straighter. Suddenly it seems possible. I can change my setting. I don't have to be stuck on the old one. Maybe I have already changed.

"Come on, Jess. Tell me the truth. Tell me what you want."

I look at this beautiful boy who's looking straight at me, so hopeful, and it hits me how ridiculous I'm being. Am I brave enough to say what I want? And try for it? Any one of us can be gone in a day, like Iona. There are no guarantees. I should know that by now. Life's too short, and you don't know what's around the corner. But tonight, he's here and so am I, and I can't think of a single reason not to grab that with both hands.

So I do. I grab him with both hands. My gold medal.

"OK, Liam Caffrey, you're on." I gather the warm cotton of his T-shirt and gently pull him toward me. Then I kiss him.

"Finally," he says afterward.

"Next, I need a drink." I start asking for what I want. I need to get into the habit. "And then we should dance."

 EPILOGUE

Christmas Day • 11:48 a.m.

Snow on Christmas Day? Like that ever happens! Only it has.
Snow so deep, each branch has a thick white crust. Even under
the trees, against the pure-blue sky, this icy lacework is dazzling. I love running in snow and today I get to try out my
Christmas presents: all garish high-vis running gear, because
Mum still hasn't lost the habit of wanting me safe and seen.
The shock of the frozen air when I leave the house is like inhal-
ing needles. But now that I'm warmed through—my fleece tied
around my waist, gloved hands pumping—I'm high with it.
The cold and the whiteness make me giddy. I run on the road,
where it's been plowed and gritted into a fine bronze slush, with
snowdrifts like cresting waves either side, chest-high now that
I'm out of the valley.

Each breath is like a miracle. I'm here. I'm alive. I made it.
Today I want to yell it from the highest hill. Last Christmas
seems light-years ago. I'd like to think that was the lowest point
of my life, but it doesn't work like that. No guarantees. I don't

know what's waiting. The difference is, now I believe I can survive it.

I reach the top of the hill and turn left on the long straight road to the chapel. You can see for miles, over to the tiny dark stub of the Pike on the far hill. There's a dirty yellow snow cloud approaching from the west, smudging the horizon to an ashy blur. More snow soon, then.

I see a spot of bright cherry red. Eden! She's coming up the bridleway in her padded ski stuff, hat, and gloves: Must've been a battle in these drifts, but I think that's part of the point.

"Hey! Happy Christmas!" I shout, breathless, running to meet her.

"Happy Christmas!" She hugs me tight and then pulls back, scanning my face carefully.

I do the same. We can't help it, I think, after everything. We constantly check the other is OK. I smile and tug my fleece on again so I don't get chilled, then we turn to trudge the last half mile together.

"So. First Christmas since Steph moved in," Eden says. "How's that working out?"

"Yeah, it's not bad actually. Mum laughs way more. Plus, Steph's a better cook. Christmas dinner was shaping up nicely as I left, ta very much. Home-made Christmas pudding—we never had that before!"

"All good, then? Your mum deserves it."

"All good." I nod. "Steph even backs me up, sometimes, when me and Mum fight. Wasn't expecting that." Then I laugh. "You wanna know the downside? Promise you won't tell anyone?"

"Course, J. What?"

"PMS week in our house is hell. I'm not even joking. Three of us in sync. Can I move in with you next time?"

When she's finished laughing, I ask, "So, are you seeing Tyler later?"

"I might be. If this snow doesn't put him off walking up our hill. Southerner! He's not used to it."

"Still going well, then, you two?"

She grins. "Yep. We had a good start, weird to think of it now. We kind of fast-forwarded somewhere, me and him. He got under my skin. He knows I'm not *nice*, and it's such a bloody relief. He sees through me, J, in a good way. And I let him in. He's OK. I mean, yeah, he's got swagger, but really, he's solid, I promise."

"OK. If you say so, I believe you. But be careful, E. If he hurts you, I will be coming for him. You can tell him that."

I'm so fierce I can see she wants to laugh, but she reins it in. "OK, I'll pass that on. You seeing Liam today?"

"*I might be . . .*" I repeat her words, and we nudge each other, giggling, but there's something accepted, about our lads and how we feel about them.

"Anyway, he's only four streets away, so no excuse. Plus, he's supposed to be helping me with the framing. Deadline's straight after the holidays."

"That's good. You deserve this, Jess."

I still can't believe it, but I've got my own exhibition. Just a little shop in town, but I have to sort and frame all the prints I've chosen. These last few months, the painting's been so good

I've got more than I need and I can be choosy. My portfolio is growing fat. I've emailed Aisha for one of my art-college references. There's a future taking shape, still blurry, but so bright I hardly dare look at it.

We don't speak for this last bit. Eden pushes the old iron gate open over smooth compacted white. We're not the first to do this. You can see at a glance which graves have had their Christmas-morning visit. Iona's row is deep, pristine snow, but we break a path to her through the thick, powdery drift.

I wait and let Eden go first.

She takes off her hat and gloves and unzips her backpack.

"Hey, Iona. Happy Christmas." Eden takes out a bit of holly and sticks it in the snow at the base of the headstone.

IONA HOLBY

1998–2016

BELOVED DAUGHTER, SISTER, FRIEND

"Here you are." She places a mince pie on the top of the stone. Next she reaches into her pocket, pulls out a miniature bottle of brandy. She takes a swig and hands it to me.

I copy her—coughing on the hot burnt-sugar flavor—and pass it back.

She sprinkles it. Amber drops melt the snow where they land.

"Do you remember when we studied Mexico, and the Day of the Dead?" Eden asks without looking at me. "How they party with their dead people, bringing them food and drink? I liked that idea, even back then, before I knew any dead people."

She sits back on her snowy boots.

"The grief counselor says it's OK to admit it all. Bad stuff. Good stuff. That we fought. That I loved her. That we were friends once."

"Course it is."

"She said grief is just love with no home. I get that. The love doesn't stop just because the person has. But I felt like a hypocrite, you know, for being sad? Like she'd chuck it in my face if she knew: *You? Sad? You hated me! I thought you'd be glad I'm dead!* And you know the worst thing? For one split second the day she died, I *was* glad. Glad the fighting was over."

"That's got to be normal. Don't beat yourself up."

"Oh, but I do. I'm good at that. The mad thing is, right now I would literally give my right arm to see her again. Even if it was just one last time. To hug her and say sorry would be . . ." She gulps on the tears.

I crouch next to her in the snow. Give her some time. I can feel the compacted cold seeping up. "How's it been, today?"

"It's hideous, but I was ready for that, first Christmas and all. It couldn't be more wrong. It's like we're unbalanced—a chair with one leg missing—so we're all useless and crooked and tipping over. We just don't work."

I go with her image. "Maybe you have to get broken down and built into something else."

"What if I don't want to be? I don't want to get used to it, Jess, but I can feel it happening." She's crying proper tears now, plopping off her chin and into the snow.

"It's still terrible, worse than you can imagine, but it's not constant. Not like it used to be. It's lifting, just a little. It's like losing her even more. I can still picture her, though." She closes her eyes. "She could be standing right there." She waves a hand to her left. "I can see her, Jess, smirking down at me, for doing this."

I blink twice. I see her too.

Iona, in her winter coat, laughing at us. Her fair hair is loose in the wind. Her cheeks are as pink as ours. "Holly and brandy? For me? I'm honored. Cheers, girls." She raises one hand in a salute. Then she turns on her heel and disappears just as the first flakes of snow start to fall.

Eden opens her eyes, exhaling long and slow. She pats the headstone. "We'd have made up, one day. And just 'cause we didn't get time, it doesn't mean I have to get stuck on the bad bits."

I get that. I was stuck for a while there too. Stuck in pain and fear. Too stuck to speak up and be seen. "It's OK. We can be the walking wounded. I reckon that includes everyone, sooner or later." My hair is escaping, so I tuck it behind my ears. Even my damaged one is good for that.

She gives me a little crooked smile, wiping her face. "Hey, your ear," she says, noticing. "You stopped hiding it."

"Yeah, I reckon what other people think, that's their business, not mine." It's taken more counseling, but on my good days I can just about pull it off.

"When did you get so wise?" Eden asks.

"Right back at you." I say it so it lands as gently as these new snowflakes.

Eden is putting gloves back on. "Come on, Jess." She starts scrabbling around in the drift by her feet. "Let's make her a snowman. She always loved them. When we were little, we made a massive one on the front lawn, proper face and everything." She's already rolling a ball.

So I help her. There's a hysterical edge to our laughter, but we commit to the task. We make a respectable snowgirl, just to the side of Iona's grave—at the end of the row, in the vacant plot. I shape her head with care. I give her one perfect ear and one that's angled, to match mine. We find stones and leaves for her mouth and eyes, little sticks for her arms.

"There," Eden says to Iona's headstone, "so you have company today, OK?"

I see Claire's car appear in the distance, slowly driving toward the chapel. "Hey, your folks are here. I'm gonna leave you to it, OK? Say hi to them for me, yeah?"

"Same to your mum and Steph." She nods.

I leave Eden there and wave at Claire and Simon as I pass their car. I set my chin, shoulders back, deep breath, and I start running home.

The view is better this way, an expanse of pale valley and the enormous domed sky, as if the world is a snow globe. Looking around me, I see this snowy world's not black and white at all. It's full of color.

That holly tree is swathed in shadows of plum and cobalt. Its leaves are glossy wintergreen spikes, hiding scarlet berries. The snowfield to my right is a watercolor, washed with apricot, violet, rose. I turn down the lane, banked high in drystone walls, coal black but veined in gold. I see a rock face hung with tiny icicles, glistening with opal fire. There's a necklace of rainbow lights garlanding the farm over there, pulsing like my heartbeat. That's three new paintings right here. I plan them in my head, excited.

I run faster, gulping down the colors. I eat them up. I make them mine. I imagine my insides: a fiery swirling palette. Then I exhale it all as dragon breath, pearly clouds in a muted seaglass sky. I laugh out loud and keep the beat going, running through color all the way into town.

The streets are almost empty. Sound is muffled. Cars are slow. Outside the park gates, there's a tall figure in a moss-green coat, making a snowball in his mittened hands.

Liam turns and lobs the snowball at me, leaving me time to duck. His laughing eyes in the bright snow light take my breath away. He catches me and pulls me close. "You're hot!"

"Why, thank you!"

"Yeah, all right, both ways!" Then, serious, "How was it up there?" He gestures at the hill I've just run down. "Are you OK?"

"I am," I say. And I stand on tiptoes in my new running shoes to kiss him.

 # ACKNOWLEDGMENTS

Writing these thanks is something of a dream come true, so please bear with me if it gets a bit Oscars-ish. First of all, I must thank Ben Illis at the BIA, literary agent extraordinaire, for his belief in my writing, even through the tough years. Ben, thank you for not giving up on me! And thanks to the rest of #TeamBIA, the most gorgeous, generous, and talented bunch of writers you could ever hope to meet. Thank you also to Ben's international colleagues Adrian Weston and Marinella Magri.

A very close second, I need to thank everyone at David Fickling Books. What an extraordinary team of people. Your enthusiasm for my story means more than I can say. Thank you, Bella Pearson, David Fickling, Phil Earle (I'm so glad you moved to Hebden Bridge), Simon Mason, Bronwen Bennie, Carolyn McGlone, Anthony Hinton, Alison Gadsby, Talya Baker, and last of all (but actually first and foremost), Rosie Fickling, who stayed up late to read my story on the day it arrived: Thank you so much.

This novel was written as part of my PhD in creative writing, so next I must thank my wonderful team of supervisors at Leeds Trinity University, especially Martyn Bedford (a mentor with the perfect combination of understanding, humor, and rigor), Susan Anderson, Paul Hardwick, and Garry Lyons from the University of Leeds. Without your guidance and the support of the studentship from LTU, I couldn't have written this book.

Thank you to Tara Guha for reading this story (and the ones that came before) and for your friendship all along. Thank you, Janine Bullman. Thanks to Anne Caldwell and Andy Leigh for the coaching. Thank you, Stephen May and the Monday night writing group. Thanks also to Beverley Ward and to Writing Yorkshire for the free read from TLC when this was just a half-formed idea.

Thank you to everyone who helped with my research. Any mistakes here are mine, not yours. Thank you to Sue Whitehouse and to Andy Manns MCSFS, a CSI with the Avon and Somerset Constabulary, for helping me with police procedural information. Thank you, Dr. Finian Black for your advice about head trauma treatment. Thank you, Anna McKerrow, for the tarot reading and advice. Thank you, Dr. Andi Johnson-Renshaw, for your guidance on young-adult psychology and PTSD.

A special thank-you is owed to Arvon and to all the colleagues and writers whom I met at Lumb Bank, the Ted Hughes Arvon Centre, over the four years I worked there. I hope the story is full of the great love I hold for that unique place. Thank you to the incomparable ladies of Lumb: Bec Evans, Rachel Connor, Ilona Jones, Jill Penny, and Becky Liddell. And thank you to all the fabulous Arvonistas, past and present, including

Ruth Borthwick, Claire Berliner, Becky Swain, Dan Pavitt, and Pete Salmon (who's probably forgotten I still owe him a bottle of whiskey). I don't think I would have kept writing without the support and advice of the writers I met at Arvon. Thank you especially to those who read my work and encouraged me: Steve Voake, Tiffany Murray, Maggie Gee, Jonathan Lee, Julia Golding, Celia Rees, Marcus Sedgwick, and Nicky Matthews Browne.

To my first actual young-adult readers, massive thanks and respect. It was a scary thing to share my work with you, and you were so kind and generous with your feedback. Holly Illis and Elisha Cruthers, I salute you.

Huge thanks and gratitude go to Melvin Burgess and Brian Conaghan, for your early support, vast generosity, and the cracking testimonials. What can I say? You're gentlemen and superstars and masters of this craft.

OK, here I start sniffing a bit. Thank you to my dear friends Helen, Lee, Vic, Nicky, Tash, Sue, David, Alex. Yvonne, I really wish you were here to read these thanks. Likewise Ben. Mum and Dad, thank you for everything. Thank you to Matthew, Sian, and Alex; to Eileen, John, and Jonjo; to Uschi and Uli; and to my cousin Sarah Mason for all the beautiful photography (sarahmasonphotography.co.uk). Thank you to my astonishing and beautiful daughters, Molly and Hanna. And finally, the biggest love and thanks to Christoph, who has believed in me for a very long time now.

# ADDITIONAL
INFORMATION

This is a work of my imagination. I've taken liberties with real-life geography, and the people described are fictional.

I wrote the book from a place of empathy and solidarity for anyone who has experienced a hate crime, and in the UK, where I live, this includes criminal activity against an individual because of prejudice against their lifestyle or dress code. There are far too many real-life stories involving hate-crime attacks, and I don't try to speak for anyone else. For more information and support if this story has affected you, here are some organizations whose work you might be interested in.

The National Crime Prevention Council
http://www.ncpc.org/topics/hate-crime/tolerance

The National Crime Prevention Council offers advice and resources for building tolerance among teens.

Partners Against Hate
http://www.partnersagainsthate.org/

Partners Against Hate offers advice for families and young people: "By helping our children to recognize and talk about discrimination, we help them to become adults who will work to end it."

The Dougy Center—The National Center for Grieving Children and Families
http://www.dougy.org/

The Dougy Center provides support and training locally, nationally, and internationally to individuals and organizations seeking to assist children in grief.

The American Foundation for Suicide Prevention
https://afsp.org/find-support/

"Bringing hope to those affected by suicide"—The American Foundation for Suicide Prevention provides contact numbers, links, advice, and resources.